CREATURE OF LAKE SHADOW

MICHAEL COLE

SEVERED PRESS
HOBART TASMANIA

CREATURE OF LAKE SHADOW

Copyright © Michael Cole

WWW.SEVEREDPRESS.COM

ISBN: 978-1-922323-21-7

CHAPTER 1

Karl Wickard clenched his teeth as he eased on the brake. The 33,000-pound propane bobtail truck, despite its weight and power, was no match for the ferocity of mother nature. The wheels spun against the ice. He could feel the slight shifts from left to right; the symptom of a vehicle with no traction. Snowfall peppered the windshield, making the world around him as white as the truck he was operating. The road was narrow, surrounded by an army of barren trees, all covered in thick snow.

In the back of his mind, he cursed the winter storm that blanketed the state in snow and ice. Of course, *now* was the time that the only two clients with properties out here were due for their propane deliveries. But, though he wanted to, he couldn't blame them; after all, they weren't in control of the weather. And with the temperature getting so cold, it would not be good to be without power.

"I should've stuck with accounting," he muttered to himself. He never cared for truck driving, especially the longer hauls. He passed truck-driving school by the skin of his teeth and had never really grown used to operating such a large vehicle. Even the bobtails, which were much smaller than tractor trailers, were not his cup of tea. Every day, he tried to use these jobs as motivation to get himself back to college. Then again, he was getting failing grades long before he dropped out, and that was not due to stress of life. Just laziness.

He felt a tap on his right shoulder.

"Dude, you tense up any more, you'll be squeezing out a turd," Fredrick said. Fredrick was seven years older, and much more confident. He took more of a liking to the job than Karl, and after working eleven years in the company, he was content. Glancing at his buddy, Karl saw another reason he didn't want to stick with driving. Sitting for eleven years with no exercise in-between, the thirty-five year old Fredrick Marsh had lost all trace of his youth. Formerly attractive facial features were buried under a bristly beard, and the abs that girls loved in his college years were lost under a near-sagging belly.

"Just let her slow down. Easy… there you go."

At least he's patient, Karl thought. He untensed as he regained control of the vehicle.

"I just want this over with," he said.

"You keep driving like that, we'll be long from over with. We'll be trapped in a snowbank instead," Fredrick said. "We're ten miles from town already. And you know how it is there. Nobody will want to trek all the way up into Circle Mountain to haul a couple dumb truckers out. It's a pain on a good day, but in this weather? Forget it. And we *definitely* can't count on dispatch for help. Not with the weather that's coming."

"*Hence*, I want this to be done and over with," Karl said. He had seen the forecast. By late afternoon, a massive cold front would be rampaging through the Midwest. Forecasters predicted over twelve inches of snow and winds up to thirty miles per hour.

Luckily, the snowfall was light at the moment. But that damned ice—he swore, hell wasn't a place of fire, but freaking ice!

"We'll be long gone before that," Fredrick said. He took a sip of coffee from his thermos. "Besides, we're getting paid by the hour. So just take your time. We only have another ten miles to go."

"Oh, that's comforting! Urgh! Why do these guys feel they need to live miles from civilization like some mountain man?" Karl complained.

"I don't know. Probably the reason you just described?" Fredrick said. "Besides, they don't *live* up there. These are cabin properties. Getaway places. As far as I know, there's not many people up in these parts as there used to be. Just Mr. Schroeder's cabin and one other near the other side of the lake. Not a lot of people go up there, except maybe to fish once in a while in the summer. I suppose it's a good place if one wants peace and quiet. They pretty much rely on propane-powered generators for electricity." He leaned forward and gazed at the trees as Karl drove around a bend. The elm, birch, and maple trees had shed their leaves, their barren bodies looking possessed as they waved in the wind. The pine trees were packed with snow, nearly resembling an army of giant snowmen.

It was the fifteenth time that Fredrick had made this run. He always thought Circle Mountain should've been called something like 'Bowl Mountain', because that's how he would describe it. It was a circular series of hills and rock ledges that surrounded a depression where the lake was. From high above, it looked like a salad bowl.

I guess Circle has a better ring to it.

A huge clump of snow fell from the high branches of a tree and splattered all over the windshield, making him jump. Karl jumped too, nearly swerving off the road.

"Whoa, careful there!" Fredrick said. Karl slowed the truck to a stop, then caught his breath.

"I hate this job," he muttered.

"Just get us there and back in one piece, then you can go home and curl under a blanket," Fredrick said.

"Don't know why you don't drive," Karl said.

"Because it was assigned to YOU!" Fredrick exclaimed. "I was nice enough to tag along and make sure you don't get lost."

"There's only one road. I'm not concerned with getting lost..." Karl groaned. He eased on the accelerator and continued the perilous journey. He glanced up, watching the trees swaying in the wind. High above them, the sky was grey. Far to the north, the clouds were darker, the first wave of the misery that would soon swallow the area. "...It's getting out."

Fredrick leaned back in his seat and looked at his phone. As usual, his phone failed to get a signal. Thus, the GPS failed to work. Luckily, he knew the route by heart. As he had stated to Karl, it was a simple route to begin with.

"We have time," he said again. They continued following the road as it bent to the left, taking them deeper into the dense forest.

****

After several miles, they came to a fork in the road. Following Fredrick's instructions, Karl carefully steered left toward Mr. Schroeder's cabin, tensing as the road led them down a small hill. Immediately, he nearly lost control. The vehicle was hugging the right a little too far. Karl turned the wheel to the left but was too late. The truck jolted as the front right bumper grazed the side of a tree.

"Fuck!" he muttered, steering the truck away.

"Nice one," Fredrick muttered.

"Sorry," Karl said. He was cringing. As much as he hated this job, he was still terrified of losing it. The bills didn't pay themselves.

"Eh," Fredrick shrugged his shoulders. "Not your fault. These roads are shit to drive on. Stop a sec and let me take a quick look." He stepped out and gave the damage a brief glance, then stepped back in. "Lost a small chunk of bumper."

"I didn't hit it *that* hard," Karl said, defensively.

"I didn't say you did," Fredrick replied. "This truck's old. That bumper's been hanging by a thread for at least a year. She doesn't look too beat up beyond that." He rubbed his hands together then sipped his coffee to warm up from the brief but unpleasant moment in the freezing wind. "Let's get going."

"You got it," Karl said. There was relief in his voice. That relief didn't last long, as he slowly eased the truck down the hill.

A series of bends followed. He kept the truck at a steady pace of thirty miles per hour. He did not want to risk any more close calls. With no cell signal and poor radio reception, getting stuck would be their worst nightmare.

"Hopefully this guy loves his cabin out here in the woods," Karl said. "Once this storm hits, he's gonna be stuck there for a while. I don't get the impression they plow these roads much."

"No, they don't," Fredrick said. "One thing I've noticed about the townsfolk, they don't like coming out here much."

"Not even in the summer?"

"No."

"Shame," Karl said. "Despite my complaints, I have to admit, this area's gotta be a beauty in the spring and summer. Why don't they come out here? Is it all private property?"

"Other than a few acres around the cabins, it's open to the public as far as I'm aware," Fredrick said. "It's weird. It's almost as if they're afraid of something. For the last twenty-odd years it's been that way. Since..." his voice trailed off.

"Since what?" Karl asked.

"The word is a meteorite crashed somewhere in these parts," Fredrick said. Karl glanced between him and the road.

"A meteorite?"

"Yeah."

Karl's nervous demeanor turned into a loud burst of laughter.

"They're afraid of a meteorite? What, do they think there was an alien inside it?" In his laughter, he lost focus on the road. The truck hit a patch of ice, ending his merriment in the blink of an eye.

"Whoa!" Fredrick said. Karl clenched his teeth as he fought for control. The truck skidded left a couple of feet, then gained traction. Both men blew a sigh of relief. Karl's fear of driving had returned to him.

"My bad," Karl said.

"We're almost there," Fredrick said. "Just take us around this bend. It should dead-end in a half mile or so at the guy's driveway."

They drove a few minutes in silence. Karl kept his eyes on the white snow that blanketed the concrete. More of it had fallen from the trees, hitting their hood and windshield. He put the wipers to work, brushing clumps of white powder off the glass. As the snow trickled off the sides, he found himself staring off into the woods. The space between the trees was barren. There was not an animal in sight. No deer. No squirrels or rabbits. An area as untouched as this should be booming with wildlife, even at this time of year. He hadn't seen a single thing up till now.

"You were saying something about a meteorite…" he said.

"I don't know," Fredrick said. "These are country folk. They're weird. Though…it's said that these woods used to belong to more people. It was like a vacation resort. A number of them disappeared without a trace, and the rest left. Even the crews that tore down the houses claimed they saw something watching them."

"Something? What do they mean, *something*? Sasquatch?" Karl asked, letting out a nervous chuckle.

"Who knows?" Fredrick said. "Like I said, I think it's weird superstition. These people out here live in their own world."

"Gotchya," Karl said.

He carefully accelerated up another hill. It took him several hundred feet until he reached the peak. As the road bent to the left, he spotted a small clearing in the woods. He could see the iced over surface of the lake. It was a medium-sized lake, with an odd shape resembling a half-mile wide bacteria cell. Thin tidal waves of snow danced in the clear space above it as the wind kicked into action.

He eased down the other side of the hill, passing several yards of thick trees. The road narrowed as it neared the lake. Then finally, a space formed between the trees. He saw the back of the two-story cabin which faced out toward the shore. There was a Dodge pickup truck parked along the side of the building, its hood and windshield covered in snow.

Karl had to apply extra pressure to get through the lumps of snow in the driveway.

"Nice of the guy to shovel for us," he groaned.

"It's a little strange. He usually does if there's snow," Fredrick said.

"He's probably tucked in nice and cozy inside," Karl said.

"I don't know…" Fredrick pointed around the back of the cabin. A series of tracks led from the front around to the back. "Those look new."

Karl steered around the back of the cabin near the large propane tank, then parked.

"Let's get this over with." He stepped out and started prepping the hose. He unscrewed the cap on the storage tank and attached the connector. As he stretched the hose out from the truck, he glanced down at the tracks which were nearby. They continued on into the woods. He found himself studying their size and shape. They weren't leading to the woods...they were coming *from* the woods. "Hey, Fred?"

"Yeah?"

"You don't happen to know Mr. Schroeder's boot size by any chance, do ya?"

"How the hell should I know?"

"I mean...uh, is he a big guy?"

"No. Not much taller than you," Fredrick answered. Karl was a short guy, only a hair over five-foot-six. If what Fredrick said was true, then these enormous tracks did not belong to the cabin's owner. Whatever had left them was at least seven feet tall and built like a wrestler. Hell, maybe even eight feet. And even if they were from a big man, it didn't explain the jagged extensions at the toe of each print. There were two of them, shaped like the horns of a bull. And judging by the shape in the lump, they were curved downward like cat claws.

Fredrick approached with a clipboard containing the paperwork and glanced down at the tracks. He stared for a moment, understanding Karl's confusion and apprehension.

"Something from a generator or power tool, maybe?" Fredrick said. His attempt to rationalize what he was seeing failed. He wasn't sure what could make such large and bizarrely shaped tracks. *Were they even footprints?* They were spaced out as such. And, like Karl had noticed, they appeared to have come from the woods. "Like you said, let's just get this over with."

Fredrick walked around the front of the log cabin, watching the tracks as he went. There were signs that whatever created them had stopped. The snow had been stirred in some places, as though something had stopped and inspected the outside wall. To complement that suspicion, there were markings on the cabin. The wood had been scraped and splintered in some places.

"The hell?" Fredrick continued around the corner. "Mr. Schroeder?! Hello?! Sir, it's Woodward Propane, here to deliver your..."

He cleared the corner and saw the porch. Streaks of red had melted the snow and coated the porch under the awning. Those strange tracks led right up to the porch, and by the looks of it, had continued inside. He saw the door wide open...

Fredrick took a closer look, taking precautions with each step.

The door wasn't just open, it had been ripped from its hinges. The door frame was splintered, with an entire chunk missing from the top. The door was several feet inside, broken into multiple fragments. Fredrick looked at the red that was at his feet. It was blood, which had only recently gone cold. Whatever occurred, it didn't happen long ago. In fact, they just missed it.

His mind screamed at him to jump into the truck and hightail it out. Against his better judgement, he slowly approached the patio and peeked inside.

The living room and kitchen were one big room taking up the front of the building, with steps leading upstairs through the back wall. Fredrick grew lightheaded. Plates and coffee cups were smashed along the kitchen area. The tile floor was ripped up, as though put through a wood shredder. On the living room floor was a pool of blood, dark red and thickening from exposure. Nearby, a fire axe lay on the floor, its wood handle smeared by bloody handprints.

His eyes went to the fireplace. First, he saw the shreds of clothing. Then something else...something round, covered in blood. Fredrick froze as he saw the lifeless eyes of Mr. Schroeder's severed head staring back at him from the floor. Strands of meat dangled from the stub where his neck had been. The jaw was slack, the teeth inside broken.

Fredrick shrieked and stumbled backward, hitting the porch rail on his way out. He teetered on his back, falling headfirst into the bloody snow. He rolled onto his stomach and pushed his hands against the ground to stand up. His glove hit something rigid. He lifted his hand, seeing the sleeve of a severed arm that had been buried in the snow.

Fredrick leapt, screaming "Jesus, GOD!"

After hearing his friend's yells, Karl dropped the hose and ran around the front of the cabin. He quickly saw Fredrick in hysterics. He was prying his gloves off, his face displaying fright and disgust, as though he had touched biohazardous material. Then Karl saw the blood and the arm.

"What the hell?! What's going on?!" He started looking around, watching between every patch of trees. "Who...what...?" He wanted to ask, 'what did this?' but the words failed to escape him. Fredrick fumbled into his coat pocket to grab his cell phone. He immediately dialed 9-11, then held the phone to his ear. He heard no dial tone.

"Goddamn, stupid trees!"

"Fuck making a call! Let's get the hell out of here!" Karl said. He was already backing up toward the truck. Fredrick waited another moment with the phone at his ear. It was useless. He wouldn't be able to get a call out until they got closer to town.

"Let's go," he said. They hurried to the truck.

"Shit!" Karl said. "I got the hose hooked up to the tank."

"Then get it off! Hurry up!" Fredrick was shouting. A gust of wind blew some snow from the trees onto the men. It clung to their faces and jackets like glitter while they converged on the propane tank.

As they worked to remove the hose, Fredrick noticed the tracks again. Except, these ones weren't here before. They appeared to have come from the woods, had passed by the tank…going toward their truck.

He heard a hissing sound, reminding him of a snake prepped to strike. Fredrick felt himself quiver as he felt the presence of something behind him. Karl, on the other hand, proceeded to work. He removed the hose and brought it back to the tanker, oblivious to the new evidence as he hurried to the truck's winch. He saw his senior co-worker frozen in place, looking at the ground. Finally, Fredrick slowly turned to face him.

"Come on! What are you waiting for?!" Karl saw the horror in Fredrick's face. At that moment, he realized he wasn't looking at him, but *past* him. He felt hot breath brushing the back of his head. The hair on the back of his neck stood on end. That's when he noticed the fresh tracks leading behind the truck.

He turned around and saw it staring back at him.

It was humanoid, but there was nothing human about it. A long extended arm reached out. Karl gagged as three elongated claws punched through his body like spears.

Fredrick screamed as he saw the thing lift Karl's skewered body high into the air. His arms and legs twitched as blood drizzled from his mouth. Karl gagged once, his lungs deflated and unable to generate the breath to scream. In seconds, he went limp.

The thing had stepped around the back of the truck, eight feet in height, still holding Karl high above its deformed head like a prize. Fredrick only saw one way out. He dashed for the open driver's seat. He quickly started the engine, then started pulling the door shut.

He saw the beast stepping around the truck on jointed legs. It leaned forward; its jaw hyperextended. Before he could slam the door, something wet splattered across his face. Saliva. Fredrick locked the door and slammed on the accelerator.

Suddenly, he couldn't see anything. His face burned. The wet sensation turned to fire. The nerves in his face went into overdrive. Fredrick clutched his face. The skin had turned to goo, which proceeded to melt away from his skull. He tried to scream, but the acidic saliva had eaten through his cheeks, giving his jaw a dog-like appearance. He slammed the gas pedal, racing the truck forward blindly. It only took a few seconds for him to collide into a tree, the momentum slamming him against the steering wheel. A red pool of melted flesh and blood poured onto the dashboard, leaving a sizzling skull behind.

The glass exploded inward. Razor claws punctured the door and ripped it free. The last thing Fredrick felt was the impalement of his ribcage, yanking him free, followed by the tearing of flesh as he was pulled apart.

CHAPTER 2

It was 7:30, and the sun had yet to rise over Richardson, Kentucky. Home to seventy-thousand people, the general nine-to-five crowd were starting to take to the roads to begin the day. The streets were lit with a flood of headlights. Car horns beeped at intersections as drivers impatiently tried to rush their way to work.

It was the one thing Charles Jude enjoyed about early morning; he usually avoided the typical chaos on the road. The snow that had accumulated overnight only exacerbated people's attitudes. The car's clock blinked the half-hour mark as he parked in his marked space behind Advanced Bank. As the manager of this facility, he always arrived ninety minutes before opening. There was always work to be done before the typical daily operations of a bank. There were meetings, financial reporting, scheduling for staff, planning on operating aspects and a world of other things. He dug in his pockets for his bank keys then stepped out the car. Next was the fifteen-foot walk from his parking spot to the back entrance.

Vivian crouched low behind the dumpster. Her black pants and hoodie matched the early morning darkness that consumed her and her companions. She was breathing heavily and her hands were shaking. She peeked around the corner for the fifth time in a row, watching the bank manager step out of his car. The parking lot lights illuminated his grey suit, wire-rimmed glasses, and receding hairline. He was performing his normal routine, glancing out into the parking lot. The lights shone over most of the empty lot, their reaches ending on the front side of the dumpster.

"The hell are you doing?" Vivian felt a hand grab her by the hood and pull her back. That same hand then grabbed her by the shoulder and forcibly spun her around. He pulled back the thin black ski mask that covered his face, revealing the wrinkled features of anger that was Dillon Connors. He was ten years her senior, though he looked double that. Possibly the result of drugs, crime, and fighting. That face was marked with numerous scars, particularly on his brow just above his left eye; the result of a broken bottle in a bar fight. Those eyes narrowed, burning her with their gaze.

"You trying to screw this up?" The whisper did little to mask his intensity.

"No, I—I'm sorry. I'm just—" Vivian said.

"Shut the hell up," he hissed. Vivian clenched her jaw. She hated speaking with her ski mask on anyway. It was too tight, compacting her jaw, nose, and temples. She could see Matt Henry behind him. He was shaking as bad as she was, though his reasons were different. Dillon pulled his mask back down and subtly grabbed Matt by the back of his hair. "Same with you, Matt. You fuck this up, I swear to Christ—"

"I'm sorry," Matt said. "I'm with you. I just haven't had a—"

"You can have all the booze you want when we're done," Dillon whispered. He let him go. *God! He had to get the shakes now. Unbelievable.* He wanted to shout his fury but kept it in. There were more important things to deal with at the moment.

Dillon peeked around the corner. By the looks of it, the manager did not hear their spat. He was now walking to the back door, oblivious to the people watching him. Dillon looked across the parking lot at a large bush. Behind it was a pile of snow. At one moment, it was still. Then, it seemed to come alive, nudging back and forth like a miniature earthquake was taking place. Then, like a possessed corpse rising from the grave, a hand emerged, covered in a black sleeve and glove.

It only took a moment for Keith Buckner to free himself of the snow mound that his companions had buried him under. As far as the branch manager was concerned, that mound was already there, thanks to the landscapers plowing over the weekend. The robbers had simply dug the snow out, placed Keith in, then piled it back up on top of him. In a mad dash, he rushed the short distance between him and the manager.

"Now," Dillon announced to the others.

A tense shock ripped through Charles' body as he felt the muzzle of a revolver press against the back of his head. He knew immediately what was happening. He raised his hands and pressed his forehead to the door.

Dillon, Vivian, and Matt converged behind the manager, each carrying semi-automatic pistols in hand.

"Alright, you know the drill, Mr. Bank-man," Dillon said. "Don't give us any trouble, and you'll get to live long enough to go fully bald."

"Okay," Charles said.

"Unlock the door," Keith said. His voice was calmer and a bit more sympathetic than Dillon's. Having more self-control, he volunteered to be the one to ambush the banker, since Dillon's temper often caused him to resort to more…barbaric…tendencies.

Charles slowly lowered his left hand to the door and slipped the key into the lock. As soon as he unlatched the handle, he felt the team bum rush him into the bank, snapping the door open the rest of the way.

"Shut it," Dillon ordered to Matt. The bumbling crook turned around, nearly tripping over a duffle bag he had dropped during their stampede. He slammed the door shut and turned around, pistol shaking in his hands. Dillon grabbed Charles and spun him around to look him dead in the eye. He pressed his pistol under his chin, then spoke with a devilish voice. "Listen, Mr. Bank-man. Here's how this works; you will take us to the vault. We know the lock has a code. You know the code. You will unlock it and open it. Then you will open the jewel boxes. All of them. You will not say a word as you do it. Afterwards, you will take a seat and do nothing. Zero. Do that, and *maybe*, we won't harm you."

Keith saw the subtle but revealing shake from the manager.

"Just cooperate and you won't be harmed," Keith said. Dillon shot him a look. Despite the ski mask, Keith could still see the simmering anger that creased Dillon's face. He clearly felt as though he was being overruled. Of course, being so gung-ho, he didn't stop to think of the psychological effect of his statement. A hostage with assurance he'd be executed even if he cooperated would be more likely to cause trouble.

"Let's move," Keith said, redirecting Dillon's attention to the matter at hand. It worked. Dillon spun Charles back then pushed him forward, letting him lead the way through the rear corridors and bathrooms to the lobby. Matt was right behind them, his feet moving in a strange, diagonal galloping motion. He was giddy, despite being in desperate need of a drink. Perhaps this was how he got in the moment. Vivian was behind Keith. Her movements definitely lacked Matt's enthusiasm. In fact, she almost looked like she was going to be sick.

Vivian stopped and sucked in a deep breath. She was hunched down, gradually gaining control over the stirring in her stomach. She gasped after noticing Keith looking at her, then calmed down after realizing he wasn't Dillon. That small relief was enough to help her regain her wits.

"I'm good," she said. She clutched the firearm with both hands and followed the group.

"My office is over here," Charles said. "I need the keys to get back there."

"Then hurry up," Dillon shouted. "Only grab the keys and *nothing* else." Charles led the group into the main lobby then turned to the right. He kept his hands above his head until he reached his office. He walked around to the front and pulled the drawer open, then pulled out a large keyring and showed it to the gunmen. Dillon grabbed him by the collar and yanked him out of the office. They then crossed the lobby then behind the teller counter, which led to another locked door. Charles opened it, revealing the room with several lockers.

"Unlock all of these," Dillon demanded. Charles worked his way across the room, unlocking each box until he reached the back of the room. There was one more locked door awaiting them. He felt the gun muzzle press into the back of his head. He understood the unspoken instruction. He pressed his key into the slot and opened the door to the vault. In addition to the key, he had to type in the security code to the electronic locking mechanism.

With a dull metallic moan, the vault opened.

"All right, let's move!" Dillon shouted. He pulled Charles backward, nearly knocking him down as he pushed him toward Vivian. "Take him out and watch him! If he makes a move, shoot him." Vivian lifted her pistol and looked at Charles, hoping he would walk without being goaded. "What are you WAITING FOR?!" Dillon's angry shout nearly made her jump. She grabbed the manager by the shoulder and pressed the gun to his neck, then walked him out.

The robbers went to work, filling their duffle bags with diamonds, jewels, and most importantly, cash. They jampacked as much as they could into the bags, filling them until there was no space left.

Vivian pushed Charles until they were in the lobby.

"Wait here," she said, barely able to contain the shakiness in her voice. She shoved him downwards, making the manager take a seat on the floor. He kept still and stared up at his captor. He could see the gun quaking in her hands.

Having worked in banks for almost twenty years, starting as a teller, Charles had experienced four robberies, this one being his fifth. One thing he learned from experience and from those he read, was how to detect someone who meant business and someone who was a rookie. This group was a mixture of both, which unnerved him more.

Vivian glanced back, hoping to see Keith or Dillon emerge from the doorway. She looked at her watch. It had only been ten minutes since they'd started. She started looking to the windows, hoping that their ruckus couldn't be heard from the outside. The anxiety of committing a felony was now replaced by a fear of getting caught. Through one of the windows she could see the street. Headlights were strolling fast, the world full of people oblivious to them and their misdoings. She reminded herself that this was the reason they planned to do this so early. Keith had staked out during the previous weeks, carefully monitoring the manager's routines from a distance. Each time, he arrived ninety minutes before the bank opened, and they had at least forty-five minutes until any of the tellers would begin arriving.

It's all good, she thought to herself. *It's all good. It's all good.*

"It's all good," she said it out loud. She realized she wasn't watching the manager. He was still, hardly moving at all. Vivian listened to the back, hearing the sounds of hustling feet and the pulling of metal boxes. The anxiety was creeping back. She felt the shakes starting to take control of her body. "It's all good."

Her eyes shot to the window. A cold chill ripped through her body. In the distance were red and blue flashers. A police car!

Vivian felt herself starting to panic. Sweat soaked her ski mask, moistening the skin around her eyes. She stepped back from Charles for a closer look, keeping her head down to not be seen directly from inside, even though the lobby was still dark. The cop car was at least a block away. It was stopped along the side of the road. She saw the driver's side door open and the cop step out. In front of him was a parked SUV.

Just a routine traffic stop.

Vivian blew a sigh of relief and backed behind the counter. The sounds of running feet grew nearer.

Dillon burst from the doorway with a full duffle bag slung over his shoulder.

"Alright, let's tie him up and…"

Charles scurried back from the teller desk, his hand having reached under it. Dillon's eyes were wide and fiery. Only two reasons he'd ever known for people to reach under a table. One was to grab a gun, the other was to trigger a silent alarm. Neither was good. He reactively snatched his Glock from his belt.

"You son of a bitch!" he shouted. The manager raised his hands, surrendering, but it did no good. Dillon fired off several rounds. Vivian shrieked and jumped back as the bullets ripped through the manager's chest and shoulders, exploding out his back.

Charles hit the floor on his back. Bubbles of blood burst from his mouth as he tried to breathe. Each attempt resulted in a sickening suckle sound.

Keith and Matt ran out and saw the twitching manager on the floor.

"Dillon! What'd you do?!" Keith said.

"She wasn't watching him!" Dillon shouted. "He was triggering the alarm!" He pointed his gun at his nervous girlfriend. "This is YOUR fault!"

"Dillon, stop!" Keith said. "Come on! We've got to go, now!"

"Get the fucking bags!" Dillon snapped. There was no time to argue. Keith and Matt rushed back to the vault, zipped their bags shut, and hurried back into the lobby. Dillon shoved Vivian forward, forcing her out through the counter door toward the back hallway. They entered the dark corridor, leaving Charles' twitching body behind. Dillon continued pushing Vivian ahead of him. They quickly approached the back door. Keith saw the leader extend his arm to push the latch bar.

"Oh, shit!" Keith said. In the madness, he didn't think to grab the manager's alarm key for this back door. Even though it could be opened from inside, a key was needed to keep the alarm from triggering. "WAIT!"

Dillon ignored him and pushed the door open, triggering a ringing alarm.

"Not waiting!" Dillon snarled. They ran out into the parking lot. Keith cursed under his breath, then out loud when he saw the reflections of police flashers from around the building's front corners.

That impulsive idiot! Had Dillon not triggered the alarm, the cops would've started at the front of the building before working around to the back, which would've bought them a few precious seconds to hop the wooden fence behind the dumpster. But the idiot wouldn't listen, and the alarm would now draw them back here.

Vivian's heart was drumming hard. Even in the dark, she saw the expression in Dillon's eyes. He was wondering how the cops got here so fast. She knew better to keep the answer to herself. It was clear that the officer performing the traffic stop was the one now pulling up in front of the bank.

First, they threw the bags over the fence.

"Go!" Dillon said. Matt was the first to hop the fence, his legs like those of a grasshopper. Vivian wasn't quite as spry, probably due to her anxiety and not being driven by an urge to suck on a bottle. She grabbed the fence and pulled herself up. She was halfway over when she saw a human shadow sweep into the parking lot. A police officer had his Glock pointed at Keith.

"HOLD IT RIGHT THERE! DROP YOUR WEAPONS!"

Vivian closed her eyes. The poor cop didn't realize he had his weapon aimed at the wrong one. Dillon was like a demon in the way he turned, his muscular arms pointing his own Glock back at the cop. He fired off the rest of his magazine in rapid succession. The Kevlar vest succeeded in protecting the officer from the chest, however, it did nothing to defend against a couple rounds that found his neck and his jaw. The officer fired back, missing wide, then fell to his knees, unable to breathe. Blood soaked the snow in front of him. He tried to speak into his radio but couldn't.

Keith and Dillon hurried over the fence, knocking Vivian to the other side.

"Go!" Dillon said, snatching Vivian's pistol and giving her his empty one. Behind the fence was a small neighborhood. They ran down the street and found their parked van. Keith jumped into the driver's seat while the others piled into the back.

Several people had already stepped out of their front doors, alerted to the sound of gunshots. Some had iPhones in their hands, recording the group as they stepped out. The plan of parking their vehicle out of range from city cameras had just been rendered pointless.

"Go! Let's go!" Dillon shouted, pounding the back of Keith's headrest. Keith started the engine and started down the road. "Keep going down a few blocks and take a right!"

"I know where we're going, you psychopathic moron!" Keith said, letting his frustration fly. He felt a shake in his headrest from Dillon pointing Vivian's gun at the pack.

"You shut your mouth and drive!"

"Yeah? You gonna shoot me too? While I'm going forty miles an hour? Have me crash into another car? Not sure that suits your plan well."

Dillon retracted the weapon. "Just drive the fucking van. Get us where we need to go."

"I'm taking a scenic route," Keith said. He could see flashers far off in the rear view. The officer Dillon had shot had gotten the chance to alert the others of their getaway. With it being early morning, with several vehicles on the road, it would be relatively easy to get lost in a crowd. Still, witnesses would give the cops clues. And considering how many iPhones were on them, it was safe to assume the license plate had been recorded. Luckily, he had planned for this…well, not the killing part, but the overall scenario was the same. Only the consequences would be worse if caught.

Though Dillon was the leader of the group, Keith was the planner, and in a world of cameras and vehicle/plate/face recognition, he knew they would have to switch vehicles anyway.

He took a left and then a right, taking them out of the neighborhood of onlookers. After a few blocks, they would be at their destination.

Keith grabbed his cell phone and flipped through the contacts until he found the name *Jeff Robbin*. He hit dial and raised the phone to his ear. It rang once before Jeff Robbin answered.

"Hey, Jeff…you ready?"

CHAPTER 3

Jeff Robbin started the engine of his Chevrolet Traverse and waited, glancing at the rearview mirror for an ugly red van to turn the corner. Meanwhile, he watched as the first glow of sunlight started to peek through the tree line at the edge of the neighborhood. Sunlight wasn't what bothered him; it was red and blue flashers. Keith hadn't given much detail, but it was clear that things hadn't gone completely as planned.

Jeff watched the surrounding neighborhood around him. He was parked on the street, among several other vehicles in this small town. It was ten minutes to eight. People would soon be stepping out of their houses to leave for the day. A few had already left, oblivious to the escape vehicle that rested on the curb. There were many singles in this town. All night visitors did not draw attention from neighbors, as long as there was no disturbance. And Jeff Robbin played the part well. He slept in his car in front of the house of a single lady. In his reconnaissance, he learned she worked Tuesday through Saturday, and slept in late on her days off. He had seen one or two cars parked in her driveway in those two weeks. Especially in winter, she would not notice a stranger's vehicle parked outside. And even if she did, he was on the curb, not in her driveway. And when he left, he would just be part of the crowd headed to work. In the eyes of the public, that is.

There was one other house he was specifically watching, neighboring hers. Like the others, it was a two-story house. Its owner was sound asleep, having worked midnights 9:00-5:00 a.m. It was only a ten minute drive home from work, and he often got out early. One thing that was sure, though, was that all those lights were out within a half hour. And occasionally, Jeff would hear some intense snoring. The only thing different was the lack of a vehicle in his driveway. Normally, there'd be an old Ford E-150 parked.

It would be returned shortly.

Reconnaissance and studying patterns were Jeff's specialty. That, and shooting fully automatic weapons, stealth, demolition, and close-quarter hand-to-hand combat. But none of those skills came to much use after his eight years in the United States Army. Like many soldiers, he struggled to find his way after service. He tried a year of college but couldn't find a career he gave a damn about. His skills were good for nothing except possibly law enforcement, and a bulging disc in his lower back ruled that out as an option, as well as keeping him from re-enlisting. Private security paid too little for his liking. That's where the stubborn pride came in. He would not resort to working what he considered low-end jobs. It was one of the reasons he went into the service. Going back to that life would be a daily torture. Then again, so was a dwindling bank account.

That's when he received a call from someone named Keith Buckner. It was a name he hadn't heard since before the service, and a face he hadn't seen for even longer. They had sparked a friendship in their high school years, and as life went on, it took them their separate ways. But Keith had something to offer: money. He remembered Jeff's family owned a property several hours up in Blessing County, though they hardly attended it since the mysterious disappearances in '92. He had gone there a few times to maintain the place, mainly during the summer months. Never had he been there in the winter. But Keith's employer wanted a 'getaway' for a few weeks, and Jeff's isolated cabin was the perfect location. It didn't take long for Jeff to connect the dots. Frankly, he didn't care too much. He had seen the Federal Government conduct so many atrocities, using him as a tool, so knowing they were losing a relatively small portion of money didn't concern him too much. As long as he was paid, of course.

Finally, he saw headlights in his rear-view mirror. The vehicle was an old Ford E-150, moving slightly faster than the speed limit down the street toward him. It slowed as it approached, then pulled quietly into the empty driveway. He saw the doors open.

Jeff gave the neighborhood another brief look. Nobody outside at the moment. With no security cameras, they should go unnoticed. He backed a few feet into a driveway, then performed a U-turn, pulling up along the opposite side of the street to reduce the distance the robbers would have to trek, and risk being seen. They were careful to shut the doors quietly and walk casually to the back seats of Jeff's Chevrolet Traverse. Well, some were casual. The one named Matt Henry had an uneasy, shaky posture as he walked like a drug addict needing a fix. The largest figure in black pushed the smallest figure ahead with anger that was desperate to burst out. That large figure was undoubtedly Dillon Connors.

Jeff didn't have many kind thoughts toward Dillon, and seeing him pushing the one named Vivian only reinforced his feelings. The guy was impulsive, violent, and often let his emotions get the better of him. Worse, he hadn't made his down payment yet.

The crooks boarded the back of his vehicle. Dillon took the seat directly behind Jeff.

"Drive."

Jeff watched the group in his mirror. Despite their disguises, the discomfort was obvious in all four of them.

"What happened?"

"Nevermind! Let's go. We're in a hurry."

"There's a matter that needs to be discussed first," Jeff said. In a claw-like motion, Dillon ripped the ski mask off his face, tearing the fabric around the eyes. His short hair was in a frizz and his scarred face wrinkled with fury.

"The only matter is to put your foot to the gas pedal!"

"Jeff, can we handle this later?" Keith said, glancing back behind them. It was only a matter of minutes, if not seconds, that police would begin patrolling this area in search of a red van, which wouldn't be hard to spot.

"We had a deal," Jeff said. "Five grand upfront. You never paid me…"

"Oh, come on, man," Matt said. The short, quirky robber sounded only mildly annoyed as he dug for his flask. Dillon, on the other hand, was ready to explode.

Keith leaned forward.

"Please, man, let's do this later."

"No," Jeff responded. He kept his voice level and businesslike. "You made the deal. You agreed on the price. Five thousand upfront. Fifteen upon arrival at the destination. Also, you failed to pay the additional fifteen hundred for expenses. I had to dig into my own pocket to have those set up. So, now you owe me sixty-five hundred. So! Pay up, or no service."

"I'll show you service!" Dillon pulled his Glock and pointed it at Jeff's head. Unlike most people, Jeff displayed no fear.

"You shoot me, you're stuck here."

"I'll take your stupid car and drive myself!" Dillon snarled.

"You could. But you'd alert the entire neighborhood. It'd be a matter of time before you're caught."

"Hey, Farm Boy," Matt said, referencing Jeff's denim shirt and blue jeans. "If the cops find you here, you'll be arrested and charged as an accessory."

"Possibly. I'll just say you guys are attempting to carjack me."

"And when they ask about your supplies?" Dillon pointed to the groceries stocked in the back compartment.

"Winter getaway," Jeff said. "After all, it's my cabin."

Vivian watched as the gun trembled in Dillon's hand. His finger curled around the trigger, eager to squeeze. Finally, she tore open one of the bags and pulled out a stack of hundred-dollar bills.

"Here!" she said, handing the money to Jeff. He looked over, seeing her terrified eyes through the ski mask. He took the money and ran his thumb over the corners.

"You wanna count it?" Matt asked.

"This'll do," he said. He stuffed the money into his jacket. He glanced back again. "You, Vivian, sit up here. Take off that sweater and mask first. The rest of you, stay as low as you can. It's best you don't be seen for a while. Try not to get too cramped. We have about a five-hour drive ahead of us." Vivian quickly took off the mask, her long white hair flying over her face. She took off her thick black hoodie and replaced it with a flannel jacket, then moved up into the front passenger seat.

"Why does *she* get to be seen?" Dillon asked.

"It'll be hard enough to keep three of you hidden. At least she and I up front can pass as two lovers going on vacation." Dillon exhaled sharply, then leaned back.

"I guess I see your point." He put a blanket over himself and kept his head away from the window. "Don't get too cozy up there."

"Speak for yourself," Jeff retorted. Vivian sat beside him and straightened her hair. Her skin was golden, her physique a fit one. He glanced at her hands, seeing them trembling on her lap. As she rubbed her wrists, she peeled back the cuffs of her sleeves, revealing a tattoo of a shark on her left wrist. If anything was obvious, other than her good looks, it was that this whole thing was not her idea of pleasure. In fact, the look on her face indicated that she experienced something horrible. Her eyes showed signs of restrained tears. Worse, just below her neckline was an edge of purple. A bruise. Jeff took one final glance at the mirror, focusing on Dillon.

Yeah, I'm sure he had 'nothing' to do with that.

He drove down the street and took the first right. Continuing for several blocks, he finally came across some flashing lights. He could feel the group tense as one police car pulled onto the street ahead and turned toward them. Vivian looked nonchalant, keeping her eyes forward.

The cop passed by, not even giving them a glance as they made their way to the main road. He was looking for an entirely different vehicle.

Jeff pulled onto the main road and increased speed, joining a world of traffic as he took the crew north. Jeff let out a sharp exhale. It would be a long two weeks in hiding with this crew.

CHAPTER 4

"Show it to me again," the Detective said to the security analyst. They hunched at the computer desk, reviewing the security footage of the robbery. Much of it was hard to see, as the room had been dark. The Richardson City Police detective had spent his morning going through the crime scene. His men dusted for prints while the coroner had taken the bodies of the bank manager and the fallen police officer.

The officer's violent death had been felt around the department. Already, every cop was calling for blood. The news was quick to hit the public, and in less than an hour, several off-duty police had volunteered to come in to comb the streets for the killers.

Detective Gates had the unfortunate task of meeting the officer's wife and informing her of the unfortunate news. Seeing her pain only added to the motivation to have these people found. The bank would be closed for the next two days while every inch was dusted for fingerprints. Unfortunately, the perps had gloves on, and their masks concealed almost every inch of their identities. Worse, his main witness was dead. The only witnesses he had were people who spotted the crooks boarding their getaway vehicle.

For a while, he thought he had a good lead. It even led to a suspect being brought to custody. Patrols had found a vehicle matching that on cell phone videos on Shannak Street. Even the license plate contained appropriate characters that were identified by witnesses and video. However, something was off. After receiving the warrant, police raided the home and took the owner into custody. The man was sound asleep, completely confused as to what was taking place. After an interrogation, Detective Gates began to suspect that his vehicle had been stolen to be used in the robbery. A few neighbors had reported another vehicle nearby, but none retained the details of it. After all, none of them were aware of the robbery at the time, and the vehicle didn't seem out of place.

"These pricks weren't dumb," the analyst said. He winced as the video in the lobby replayed the shooting. "Well…maybe except for that one."

"Well, there's at least one smart fella in their group," Gates said. "This did take careful planning, and I'm pretty sure this guy wasn't the one to do it." He pointed at the shooter. "The lights are too dim. We can't make anything out here. Let's go to the cameras in the vault and private boxes." The analyst switched feeds. The vault was much more brightly lit, giving them much more detail of the events inside. Gates watched as the crooks moved inside, the big one violently pushing the banker along, keeping the gun pointed at all times. "That's the shooter."

"Doesn't help much," the analyst said. "Can't see any features on him." They watched quietly as the events continued to unfold. The manager unlocked the private boxes then moved to the vault. Most of the crew followed him all the way up, while one smaller figure stayed back. The analyst snickered. "Something tells me this one was roped into doing this. Just looking at his body language, he's feeling a little uneasy. Or she. It might be a she." The perp turned. "Yep, definitely a she. A pretty well endowed she."

"Wait!" Gates said. "Freeze it and go back a few frames."

"Okay," the analyst said. He froze the image and slowly rewound.

"There," Gates said, pointing. The shy robber, as she turned, had caught her sleeve on the lid of one of the open boxes. "Zoom in on that." The computer focused in on the robber's exposed wrist. There was a marking. A tattoo. The image amplified then cleared.

"A little black shark," the analyst said.

"Good. Very good," Gates said. "Let's get this out to the news, State Police, and all airports. It's not much, but it's something. And it's a specific enough marking to be a lead. Something tells me that these people have left town, but as long as we can keep them away from airports, they won't get far. Not with this winter weather we're about to get."

CHAPTER 5

It was only two hours into the trip when the snow had started to come down. It wasn't heavy, and certainly not enough to back up highway traffic. At least, not at first. As they continued north, the snow was coming down in large pellets. The sky was now a dark grey, despite only being 10:30 in the morning.

Jeff knew he could not outrun the weather. After seeing an increased number of brake lights, he knew he had to get off at the next exit. Luckily, he knew the area well, having driven here a lot before leaving for the service. The other fortunate thing was that he wasn't far from his original exit. He would travel north on this side road for an hour before finding Crook Street.

Appropriately named for the occasion, he thought.

He continued on the side road, watching the clouds roll in in the distance. Several cars were returning home, their occupants ending their work day early to endure the snow-pocalypse.

After thirty minutes off the highway, Vivian stirred from a deep snooze. She opened her eyes to see vast countryside. Much of it was farmland. There were several farmhouses with enormous barns. The properties were few and far between. It was as though she had gone back in time.

She glanced back at the rest of the crew. After getting out of Richardson, they made a brief stop to get a bit more comfortable. Dillon was in the back seat, his mouth gaped open as he slept. Matt was asleep too, his empty flask wobbling in his lap, along with an empty bag of potato chips. Crumbs were bunched in his mustache, adding to his cartoonish appearance. Keith was awake at the moment, staring out the window. It was obvious from the worry lines on his face that he couldn't sleep, his thoughts fixated on the disastrous events at the bank.

"You alright?" Jeff asked, keeping his voice soft to avoid waking the others. It wasn't him being polite, he preferred not having to listen to them banter. More importantly, during the trip he had decided he didn't want to know the details of the crime. Being an accessory to a simple robbery, he could live with. However, anything beyond that might weigh on his conscience. Unless he wasn't aware of it. And as far as he was concerned, he didn't need to be aware of it. He wasn't a suspect, neither was his vehicle.

"I'm good." She cleared her throat. "Thank you." A few moments of silence passed.

"You like sharks?"

"Huh?" Vivian asked.

"Your tattoo," Jeff said, pointing his thumb toward her wrist tattoo.

"Oh." She chuckled shyly. "Yes. Yes I love them. As a kid I wanted to be a marine biologist." That chuckle turned into a sigh. "You see where that dream went."

Jeff nodded, glancing at the group of thugs in his mirror. "Mmhmm." More silence passed for several moments. Finally, Jeff gave her a quick glance, immediately noticing her hair for the hundredth time. It was so white, it was practically lost in the snowy background.

"Interesting choice of color," he said.

"My mother did her hair like this. I used to hate it, but it grew on me after I got out of High School," Vivian said. She ran her fingers through her hair, straightening it back. "I guess we grow up to be like our parents after all. Well…in some ways."

"It's a good look. Very unique," Jeff said. Vivian smiled.

"How far do we have?" Vivian asked.

"Maybe two-and-a-half hours," Jeff said. "Weather's getting bad. Hope you guys weren't expecting a first-class comfy vacation home."

"I don't really care," Vivian said. She gazed at the window and watched the countryside stroll by. The Chevrolet was moving at a steady pace. The road wasn't too horrible. Yet. She drew in a long inhale then looked back at Jeff. He had shaved since their last meeting. Before, his face had been invaded by thick red bristles. With his expressionless bearded face and sad eyes, she almost thought of him as a wannabe wild man. But now, he had cleaned up a bit, and looked…handsome. *Really* handsome. Almost angelic in her opinion.

She redirected her gaze back to the road. She pulled down the visor and pretended to use the mirror to check her face. In reality, she was making sure Dillon was still asleep. If she was caught checking out another man, he'd lose his temper. Again. And she knew what he was like when he lost his temper.

"You want coffee?" Jeff's words interrupted her thoughts. He held up a large thermos. "It's still warm. Got some Styrofoam cups in the center console."

"Oh, no thanks," she said. "That's tempting, but I'll wait. If I drink anything at this point, it'll probably go right through me. Something tells me we don't want to take any rest stops."

"Well, not so much that," Jeff said. "It's that there's nowhere to make a rest stop for a while. At least, not until we get to town. I'm gonna need to stop at a gas station and fill up."

"Okay," Vivian said. She sat silently for a few minutes. With every passage of silence, her mind replayed the horrible murders. She needed to distract herself from them. "How old is this cabin?"

"Old," Jeff said.

"Old, as in, no hot showers?"

"Lukewarm," Jeff said. "They don't have power cables going out that far."

"Wait...There's no electricity?!"

"I have a propane generator," Jeff said. "I made an order for the tank to be filled. It should've been done this morning. The place draws water from a well. Don't expect any wi-fi. Or even television."

"Better than nothing I suppose," Vivian said. She straightened her hair again, one of her habits during anxiety. She dug into her purse and pulled a pack of cigarettes. "You don't mind?"

"No."

She put one between her full red lips and lit it. Jeff watched the strong inhales. The girl was definitely stressed.

"Nobody else lives up in this place? I forget what you call it..."

"Lake Shadow," Jeff said.

Vivian shivered. "Odd name."

"Well, the region is called Circle Mountain because of the depression in the lake. Because it's surrounded by trees, the lake is clouded in shadow the majority of the day. At least, I think that's what was on the founder's mind when he named it. And to answer your question: No. There's only one other cabin, and that's around the bend of the lake. You can't even see it from where we'll be."

"Oh, good," she said, then took another long draw. As she did, she glanced at his hands on the wheel. No ring on the left hand. No rings anywhere. At the very least, he wasn't married.

She looked back again. Dillon was still out. She wanted to sigh but didn't want to give away her emotions. In this ten-minute conversation alone, this stranger had treated her better than in the entirety of the year she had been with Dillon. She was in a world of misery, now tripled after taking part in this damned bank robbery. Dillon's way of life had been exciting...at first. She had followed him to casinos, resorts, more casinos. He loved gambling and had a few decent cash-outs, though those were all lost in his continuing gambles.

Dillon loved money but didn't want to work for it. Thus, he was no stranger to crime. He openly bragged about pick-pocketing. She knew he had mugged people in the past, and a few times they weren't together. But the individual muggings weren't doing the trick. He wanted to score large, enough to retire off of. Getting a crew wasn't hard. Matt was a drunk with no job, or life. His wife took the kids and left. He hadn't even seen them in five years. Keith was the one who was manipulated by desperation. Like Matt, he was divorced, though in Keith's case, the wife had taken over fifty-percent of his pension, his income PLUS a claim for hospital damages which she fabricated were from injuries sustained by abuse. It was all a lie, but she had a good lawyer. To add to the mix, his firm fired him, not wanting the bad reputation of having a wife-beater on their staff. Piling bills and the threat of losing a house, with nobody wanting to hire him, Keith felt like he had no way out.

It was the same way Vivian felt every time she looked at Dillon.

Finally, the group leader began to stir. He cleared his throat and coughed, then sat up. He pulled his hood back and looked around.

"Ugh," he moaned. "We there yet?"

Jeff shook his head. *Not soon enough.*

CHAPTER 6

The wind was howling by the time they reached Crook Road. The sky looked like as though nightfall was around the corner. Beneath that grey sky came a barrage of snow that seemed to last forever. The windshield wipers went to work to provide Jeff some visibility through the fogging glass.

It was a long seventy minutes before they reached the town called Ellisville. Hardly a word was spoken by the group as they gazed at the first sign of civilization they had seen for over an hour.

Civilization was one word. Probably not the first choice any first time visitor would call it. They had seen small town country before. Hell, this was Kentucky! But the houses they passed hardly looked maintained at all. Roof tiles were peeling off. Gutters dangled over cracked windows. There were even a few abandoned properties, one of which looked as though it had been left ablaze.

"The hell is this place?" Dillon said.

"Home," Keith said. "For at least two weeks. Until our new pickup meets us here."

"Hey!" Dillon said. "Careful how you let your words fly!" He nudged his chin toward the driver. Jeff saw the gesture in the mirror.

"You can rest assured your secrets are safe with me. That said, Dillon and I are in agreement for once. The less I know, the better," Jeff explained. The fact that they would be picked up in a few weeks was nothing new. That part of the plan was already in the details. Beyond those details, Jeff wanted blissful ignorance. And the cash he was owed.

The wind pounded the Chevrolet with a huge gust, sending a tsunami of snow cresting eight feet high. It hit the passenger side, momentarily blinding any view out those windows. Ice had formed along the outside, despite the heater being on full blast. Jeff looked at the thermometer. It read ten degrees, and according to the forecast, it would continue to drop into the night.

He took a turn at the next intersection, which took them into the business side of town. This part of Ellisville was a tad neater than the farmhouses they passed, yet it still looked like something from another dimension. Streetlights were hardly maintained. Only two-thirds of them were working. Traffic lights weren't functional at all. Vivian initially assumed power had been lost, only to notice that the intersections had been converted to four-way stops. Crooked stop signs marked the corner of the road, the edge of the metal bent and chipped away.

"There's the gas station," Jeff said. He pulled into the driveway, flooring the pedal to get over a huge lump of snow that blocked the entrance.

"I thought we weren't stopping for anything," Dillon said. "The whole point of this was to not be seen."

"We still have a little over twenty miles to go," Jeff said. He put his finger to the fuel gauge, which was less than a half-quarter tank. "Unless you want to be trapped out there with an empty tank."

"Well, shit," Matt said, opening his passenger door. "I need a refill anyway."

"I *really* need to use the restroom," Vivian added. She was grateful she didn't accept any of Jeff's coffee. She was close to bursting at this point.

"Hold on, everyone," Jeff said. "Not everyone go at once. As you imagine, this place doesn't get the most visitors in the world. I'm sure there's been reports of four individuals on the loose. These townsfolk might be...peculiar, but they aren't stupid. In fact, they can be bright."

"I'll go first," Vivian said. It was a statement. She had to go bad.

"Me too!" Matt said with the same conviction, though his motivation was the opposite of Vivian's.

"Pay cash for anything you buy," Jeff said to them. "And Vivian?" The girl turned around. Jeff handed her forty bucks. "Tell the clerk to fill it up on ten, please."

"Okay," she said. She took the money and hurried in. Jeff waited in the driver's seat. There was no point in standing outside. The pump wouldn't work until Vivian paid, and seeing how she was close to dashing for the front door, she would do her business before going to the counter. He kept the engine running, the heat on full blast. As they waited, he studied the parking lot. There was only one video camera, and by the looks of it, it wasn't functional. He was relieved. As far as he was concerned, the best way to handle the situation was to act as though they were America's most wanted. Then again…

His eyes went to Dillon.

…they probably weren't too far off.

Vivian washed her hands, her body finally relaxing after emptying an overfull bladder. She didn't even care that the bathroom hadn't been tended to in ages. The knob on the faucet creaked loudly as she turned it. Surprisingly, the soap had been replenished. Probably forced to do it by the Health Department.

She cleaned up and returned to the store section. The shelves were half stocked, with several of the remaining items misplaced and knocked over. The need for coffee was now tugging at her. She moved around the back aisle until she found the coffee machine. She stopped, looking disgusted at the thing. The machine had clearly not been cleaned in a week at best. And if it was, it was a minimal job, just enough to trick people into believing its contents were sanitary.

Vivian saw Matt pass her on his way to the checkout counter. Wrapped in his arms were two bottles of tequila, several bottles of bourbon, scotch, and a bottle of rum.

"Party?" the clerk said. He was a scrawny fella, with a very long mustache. His build was so skinny, it made Matt look muscular by comparison. Even more strangely, his neck was oddly crooked, like it had been broken at some point and healed on its own. The fella had full mobility by the looks of it.

What could possibly drive a place to this level of weird?

Matt, however, didn't seem fazed. If anything, the old fart was right at home.

"You can say that," he responded. "Call it, a retirement party."

"Retirement, you say," the clerk said, placing the bottles one-by-one into a paper bag. "You know what the trouble with retirement is, don't you?" His eyes locked with Matt's. It was a hard stare, almost haunting. Now Matt was feeling uneasy.

"I…I don't know," Matt said. The clerk put another bottle into the bag.

"The trouble with retirement…is that you never get a day off!"

A moment passed, then the two burst into a fit of laughter. Matt paid for the items with cash.

"Keep the change," he said, then walked out with his prized possessions. Vivian took his place. In her hand was the fifty given to her by Jeff.

"What can I do for you, sweetie?" the clerk said.

"Just a fill-on on ten, please," she said.

"You got it," the clerk said. He took the money from her hand, naturally seeing the tattoo peeking above the cuff of her sleeve. *Interesting design.* He felt like he had seen that somewhere. He didn't press the subject. "You celebrating retirement too?"

Vivian looked out the window. The snow was coming down even harder. The wind was blowing it into tornado like forms, completely burying the roads.

"Not exactly," she said.

"Yeah, you're a little young. You'll get there," he said. "Anything else I can do for you?"

"Just the gas," she said.

"In that case, be careful on the roads. The weather's not being too friendly today."

"No, it's not," Vivian cracked a nervous smile. She turned and left, trying to move as fast as possible. This whole place made her uncomfortable. Or maybe it was the stress of being on the run. Or being stuck with Dillon. Either way, she was feeling increasingly uneasy.

Jeff started filling up as soon as he saw her exit.

"Finally," Dillon said. He stepped out and marched toward the store.

"What are you..." Jeff's words were nearly lost in the wind.

"Gotta piss," Dillon called back.

"Damn prick," Jeff muttered to himself.

"Can't hold his drink," Matt joked. His smile stopped. "Oh, damn it. I gotta go too."

"You were just in there!" Keith said.

"I was focused on other things," Matt said.

"You're waiting," Jeff said, peeking through his open door.

"What?! You can't..."

"Shut your chug hole," Keith said. "Let's get out of here. Get a few miles into the country, then we can make a piss stop. Where nobody can get a grasp on how many of us there are."

Matt sat back.

"This is ridiculous. We're a hundred miles away from..."

"Judging by how packed those bags are," Jeff said, "and the *update* in the scenario, something tells me a hundred miles isn't enough." He looked up at the sky. "The idea of hiding out here was to keep you from being seen. Let's keep it that way."

Matt stayed silent as Jeff finished filling the tank. He sat back into the vehicle and started the engine back up. The warm air was welcome on his hands and face. It had taken almost no time for the temperature inside to drop.

After a few minutes, Dillon finally stepped out. He took his seat in the back.

"Much better," he said.

Jeff resisted the urge to speak what was on his mind. It would do no good. Scolding someone as irrational and impulsive as Dillon would only result in a confrontation. And judging by their encounter this morning, Dillon was very trigger happy. Jeff glanced at the edge of his seat, where he had a revolver concealed underneath it. Once they got to the cabin, he would be having it on his person at all times. With a little luck, he wouldn't have to use it. That, or the shotgun he kept stored at the cabin.

Jeff steered the Chevrolet out of the gas lot and brought them back on the road. It wouldn't be far before it would intersect with Line Street, which would take them far out to Circle Mountain.

Right now, the concern was getting there without getting stuck in the snow. He would worry about Dillon later.

****

The clerk watched as the vehicle left his lot and slowly moved far down the road until it was a little black speck lost in a world of falling white. He wondered where they were going. There wasn't anything out that way, except the road that led to Circle Mountain.

"Taking a vacation trip? In *this* weather?"

It was a sign of his typical boredom. There wasn't else much to do, other than clean, and wait for the next customer. And he hated cleaning. He returned behind his counter and watched the snow fall on the other side of the window.

After a while, he switched the television on. On the nine-inch screen, he watched the weather forecaster point to a bluescreen image of a massive cold front sweeping through the state.

The station switched back to news. There was talk about politics, business, a few local issues, all of which put the clerk in a snooze. He stirred as another customer came through the door. Just a typical resident, just here for gas and a case of beer. It was the main item the clerk was always up to speed on inventory.

"The hell with this weather," the customer said.

"May God strike his wrath on it," the clerk replied. He rang the order through and sent the customer on his way. As soon as the door slammed shut, the clerk was halfway back to snoozing.

The news station's logo popped up again on the screen as they began their next hour.

"Richardson Police are investigating an armed robbery that resulted in the murder of a police officer and the bank's branch manager."

The clerk yawned. He had seen this report when it first aired that morning. This early afternoon report was going through the usual motions. Victim's names and ages. Witness comments. People saying how they felt bad. Stuff that usually amounted to nothing as far as he was concerned.

"Detectives are still unaware of the identities of the four murderers. Security footage shows that there were four armed individuals, though it is possible they might have had a getaway driver. Lieutenant Gates, the detective in charge, wants the public to be aware that these people are armed and dangerous."

The screen showed a camera still of the four robbers, then it cut to an interview with the detective.

"We believe that three of these fellas are male, and the fourth is female. The only clue to her identity is a tattoo on the right wrist."

The clerk's eyes widened as they showed the tattoo of the shark.

"Holy, sweet Mary!"

He picked up the phone and dialed the sheriff's non-emergency number.

CHAPTER 7

The path to Lake Shadow was a long and unpleasant one. There was hardly any sign of the road, forcing him to rely on memory, and the general spacing between the trees to guide him. Even that was hard to see. The wind was blowing the snow almost horizontally, its whistle droning through the woods like a demonic call.

Jeff floored the pedal, taking them up what seemed like the tenth hill. The vehicle climbed slowly, barely making it over the top.

"What a great idea. Going to the middle of nowhere during a winter hurricane," Dillon said.

"Right, because Jeff controls the weather," Vivian remarked. She immediately regretted it. Her eyes immediately went to the mirror to see Dillon's reaction. He said nothing. He didn't have to. His eyes did all the speaking, and what they had to say wasn't pleasant.

The bruise she received two days ago started to hurt all of a sudden. She knew it would soon be accompanied by others before the day was over.

"How much further?" Keith asked.

"Not too far," Jeff said. He drove down a small slope, which led to a curve in the road. Jeff squinted as he tried to see through the thick wall of snow that soared in the wind, plastering his windshield. The wipers struggled, knocking off small mounds with each swing. For a moment, his vision was cleared, and he realized he had turned too far and was headed right for a tree. "Oh, shit!" He cut the wheel hard to the left, narrowly avoiding the tree and taking the Chevrolet into a snowbank.

"Nice one," Matt said, halfway through one of his bottles. Jeff ignored him and put the vehicle in reverse. The wheels spun uselessly, their traction lost in the thick sheets that entrapped them.

"Aaaaaand, we're stuck here," Dillon said.

"That's just great," Matt said.

"Any chance anyone will tow us out?"

"It's difficult to get someone out this way in *summer*. In this? What do you think?"

"Would we even want that anyway?" Vivian remarked.

"Hey, at least we won't be found," Dillon said, his veins popping from his forehead. "Nice one, Mountain Man. You've really earned that pay."

"Relax," Jeff said.

"Don't tell me to relax. We're stuck out here, miles from the nearest shelter…"

"I packed a few snow shovels," Jeff interrupted. "I just need to dig us out."

Dillon glanced behind them. There were three shovels in plain view, packed on top of the boxes of groceries.

"Oh," he said dumbly.

"Who's helping me?" Jeff said, glancing back.

"I'll go," Keith volunteered.

"Matt, go with 'em," Dillon said. Matt glanced back, drips of tequila shooting from his lips.

"Aw, come on. Can't you see I'm in the middle of something?"

"Not gonna tell you again."

Matt sighed and placed the cork back in the bottle. Keith opened the door, letting in a surge of freezing cold wind. Matt yelped as he followed his partner in crime out into the snow.

The trees towered high above him on both sides of the road. They swayed back and forth, dancing with the storm. The drunkard closed his eyes as icy pellets assaulted his face.

"Come on," Keith said, dragging him to the back of the truck. Jeff zipped his Carhart coat and opened the back. He handed a shovel to Keith, then another to Matt. He held the shovel diagonally like carrying a rifle at port arms. At that moment, a huge gust of wind ripped through the forest. He felt its grip on the curved blade of the shovel, and in an instant, it was yanked deep into the woods like a sheet of paper.

"Oops," he muttered, dumbfounded.

"Yeah, *oops*," Jeff said. "Go get it!"

Matt looked back into the deep forest, then back at Jeff, hoping he'd change his mind. He didn't. Matt looked to Keith. It was clear he wasn't going to come to his rescue; he was already busy digging the snow out from around the tires.

"Aagh," he moaned obnoxiously. The snow came high over his boots as he trekked into the tree line. The wind was at his back, tugging at his hood and pants. The forest ahead was alive with spiraling snow and the moving bodies of bushes and smaller trees. Branches cracked and fell in the distance beyond his sight, spurring him to hurry up and find the shovel.

He stumbled over collapsed twigs and branches until he was about a hundred feet into the woods. He found the shovel, already half-buried in snow. He picked it up by the end of the handle and lifted. Again, a burst of wind took it away, prying it from his drunken gasp and launching it another hundred feet in until it hit a tree.

"Shit. Damn. Shit!" He muttered, hopping over various pieces of debris. "Ohhhhh, I need a drink."

He kept going, tripping on branches, weeds, and other hazards buried beneath the snow. Finally, he reached the shovel and grabbed the handle where it met the blade.

"Not escaping this time!" he said, pulling it free. His victorious smile disappeared when he noticed a smudge of red near the edge of the blade. His eyes were glued to the sight for several seconds. It was thick as glue, dark red in color. Much like blood.

He looked to the ground where the shovel had fallen. At first it looked like a lump of snow...dark red a few inches down. Curiosity overcame the little sense he had, and he scraped the snow away with his shovel. The blade raked against something hard. He saw something come out of the mound.

Matt picked it up. A piece of branch?

The object was solid, though it lacked any kind of bark texture. It was stained red, slightly curved in shape, almost like a stake. He saw the broken end, the inner part white as the snow. He was holding a rib bone. Matt shuddered and dropped it, then looked back at the mound where he dug. He saw fur, and more thickened blood. A deer. What was left of a deer. Four legs extended from the body, two of them bent sideways in unnatural positions, exposing broken bones through the skin. Its neck, shoulders, and torso looked as though it had exploded. Skin was stretched outward, revealing a mess of broken bones in a pool of near frozen blood.

And blood and bone was all he could see. The entire deer had been opened up. Matt stared at the gaping wound. There were no organs inside.

The wind assaulted his ears, its ghostly drone unending. He shivered, not from cold, but fright. He looked at the snow around the dead deer. There were slight cavities, all placed in particular order, leading into the forest. Each of these cavities had been nearly buried in snow, which obscured their overall shape. But even a drunkard like Matt could see that they resembled footprints.

He started backing up, now clutching the shovel with both hands like a baseball bat. Already, the wind nearly took it from him a third time. Matt was jolted forward, holding tight to the handle to keep the shovel from flying away. He clutched it and held the blade close to his body to shield it from the wind.

He started to turn to regroup with the others when something caught his eye.

Matt froze, his eyes locked deep into the forest of swaying branches. There was something a couple of hundred yards out, standing in the middle of the writhing array. From where he stood, he saw little more than a silhouette. Unlike the trees, the wind had no effect on it; whatever *it* was. It was shorter than the trees around it. In fact, it was possibly only a few feet taller than an average man. Not only that, but it had the basic shape of a man.

It couldn't have been! It didn't shiver, nor did it make noise. The cold didn't seem to affect it. Its arms were impossibly long to be a human's, and its shape was…strange. Crooked, was the only word Matt could think to describe it. It stood firm, arms held down at its sides, staring right back at him. Constant sprays of snow obscured any details of its 'face'.

He questioned his senses. It was probably just a small, oddly shaped tree. Yet, somehow, he felt like it was watching him.

Whatever it was, it was shrouded in snow and the darkness of the forest. Its physical details were barely discernable. Matt squeezed his eyes shut, feeling an intense need for a long drink.

Matt began to back up.

Maybe I should quit drinking…

"To hell with that!" he answered his thoughts out loud. He turned and darted back to the group. Snow pounded his face, embedding into his bristles before melting. He squinted, hardly seeing the broken branch ahead of him. Unfortunately, he didn't see it in time. His foot snagged, sending him barreling into the snow with a high-pitched shriek. He had spun at least twice before landing, his face buried six-inches into the thickening powder.

He was tired, cold, and drunk. On top of that, he was anxious. The wind did little to help. Matt lifted his head from the snow, only for his face to be assaulted by a tidal wave of snow. It scratched at his eyes like sandpaper, causing him to yell again.

He could hear something against the ground. Footsteps! They hammered the ground like drums, crunching the snow beneath them. They quickly grew louder. That thing in the woods, it was coming! Matt pushed himself up onto his hands and knees and looked ahead. There was nothing but forest. No sign of the road. He had lost all sense of direction when he fell. He looked back and forth, his eyes wide with terror. The footsteps closed in. Behind him.

Matt looked over his shoulder and saw the figure standing high above him, reaching down with two thick arms. He yelled out.

"Holy shit! What is your problem?!" Jeff yelled to him. He grabbed Matt by the shoulders and lifted him to his feet. Matt hyperventilated, staring his guide in the face for several seconds. He looked back into the woods. Nothing was there. Nothing but snow and angry trees that clashed with the wind. He looked back at Jeff, his fearful expression turning into a wide smile.

"I—" he started to laugh, "I found your shovel!"

Jeff shook his head and pushed Matt along toward the road. The SUV had already been completely dug out, as well as a space on the road to allow the tires to gain traction. Keith opened the back and placed his shovel inside.

"Thanks for your help," he said to Matt.

"No problem," Matt responded. He gave the woods one final glance, then hurried into the vehicle. Keith looked at Jeff.

"Something happen out there?"

"He just got turned around. Freaked himself out," Jeff said. "That, and the booze is messing with his head."

"Nothing new there," Keith said. They both got back into the SUV. Jeff backed up, freeing the vehicle from its entrapment, then plowed ahead.

The vehicle moved slow, but steady. The snow was thick, but not quite thick enough to keep them from moving. Not yet, anyway.

Jeff noticed Vivian's worried expression.

"Not too far to go." He looked ahead and pointed. "See there? That's the fork in the road. Only about three miles to go."

"Oh, *only* three," Dillon said.

"Hey, unless you wanna rent a hotel in town..." Jeff said.

"No, thanks. I've watched enough *Tales From the Crypt* as a kid. Don't need to live it for real," Keith joked.

He was the only one who laughed. The rest of the group were uneasy, eager to get out of the storm. Dillon continued leaning back, his hand resting on the handle of his Glock. Meanwhile, Matt continued watching the forest, tilting the bottom of a tequila bottle toward the ceiling as he filled his gullet. Keith winced. Even for an alcoholic like Matt, he was taking that stuff fast enough to fill a pool.

He must've REALLY freaked himself out.

CHAPTER 8

Jeff eased on the brake as he steered the SUV down a long hill, which led into the interior of Circle Mountain. Climbing the hills meant fighting the blankets of snow for traction. Now, his worry was to not go down too fast. If he lost control and went off the road, there'd be no stopping the SUV from colliding with a tree.

He held his breath as he slowly maneuvered the vehicle. He hardly pressed on the accelerator at all. In this high altitude, much of the snow had turned to ice, making the trip down a simple glide.

"Almost...there..." he muttered.

Vivian sucked in a deep breath, hearing a large branch snapping somewhere in the woods. Trees leaned over the road, their trunks bending as far as nature would allow. Her stomach tightened. It looked like any one of them could snap at the base and crush them all.

Finally, they reached the bottom of the long stretch and followed the road to the right. She eased up, seeing the open space of private property up ahead.

"Oh, thank God," she muttered.

"We have finally arrived," Jeff said. There were audible sighs of relief from the entire group. They were cramped, tired, frustrated, and in the case of one of them, hungover.

It was a two-story cabin, enough to house eight people. The front lawn was wide and void of trees. There were picnic tables laid out at each side near the tree line, all covered in snow. Roughly fifteen-hundred feet up ahead was the lake, completely iced over and covered in snow. A small hill split the front of the property in half. Behind the cabin was a large propane generator, with cords leading to the large propane tank that stood to the left side.

Jeff parked the SUV several feet past the tank and switched off the engine.

"Main entrance is up front around the corner," Jeff said. The group hurried and grabbed their items, which had been packed the previous night. Dillon, however, carried two of the money bags instead.

"Who gets the master bedroom?" he asked.

"Not up for debate," Jeff said. Dillon grimaced, but ultimately decided to let Jeff have his way.

"Fine."

Jeff grabbed his private duffle bag and led the group to the main entrance. There was a porch with four steps leading up to it. The wind grabbed the screen door the instant he pulled it open, nearly ripping it off the hinges. Jeff hurriedly unlocked the main door and pushed it open, revealing a large living room area. Vivian stepped in after him and gazed at the enormous fireplace. In the center of the room was a large circular rug, held in place by two three-cushioned couches, a loveseat, and a Lazy Boy chair. It was a cozy sight, making her wish she had been here under different circumstances. And with less company.

She stood still as Dillon walked past her. He took a look at the place, seeing the living room, the kitchen back behind it, along with a small dining room section. The bathroom was on the right. There wasn't much to it. A shower, bath, sink, toilet and mirror, all crammed into a five-by-eight space.

The back left corner of the living room led to a stairway. Dillon marched up the stairs, tracking snow behind him all the way up. He looked back at her.

"You coming?"

"I'll wait," she said. He gave her a glare. That bitch, she clearly didn't appreciate the life he had given her. She had all of this money now and refused to understand the stress of setting up this job. Did she not want to share a room with him? If so, he had a proper response to that.

He was about to initiate that response but stopped after noticing everyone else staring back at him. He resisted his impulsive urge to slap her across the face. She would have to have her lesson another time. Dillon continued up the stairs and glanced into the assortment of bedrooms. There were two, in addition to the one downstairs and the master bedroom. The master bedroom was at the end of the hall. Its door was open, revealing a spacious room with a large bed.

"What does that prick need all that space for?" he muttered to himself. He glanced at the other two rooms, then back at the master bedroom. At that moment, he heard Keith coming up the stairs.

"Can't make a decision?" Keith asked. Dillon looked up, listening to the snow and wind scraping against the roof. Between that, and having to sleep near everyone else, especially Jeff, ruffled his nerves.

"I'll take the one downstairs," he said. He pushed past Keith as he went down the steps.

"I think Matt's unpacking in that one," Keith said.

"He'll move," Dillon's voice echoed back.

Jeff tucked a winter hat over his ears as he went back and forth, hauling the groceries into the cabin. He was grabbing the last few bags when he heard a loud snap. His eyes went to the roadway. Wood popped loudly, accompanied by a growly whine. Then he saw it.

The tree was over a hundred feet tall, its naked branches caked with snow and ice. He watched it lean further and further, until finally, the trunk opened up near the base with an exploding *crack* that sent a volley of bark hurtling like shrapnel.

The tree succumbed to the force of the wind, falling diagonally over the road. It smashed down with a thundering boom, shaking the ground beneath Jeff's feet.

"Son of a bitch," he muttered. The crew immediately ran out of the cabin.

"What was that?" Dillon asked.

"Good thing we weren't late by another ten minutes," Jeff responded. The group looked at the fallen tree.

"That's just great," Keith said.

"We're trapped here?" Vivian asked.

"Don't you have chainsaws to chop it up?" Matt asked. "There's a shed over there behind the cabin."

"I do, but I'm not doing it while the weather's like this," Jeff said. "It'll have to wait till it clears up."

"Relax," Keith said. "We've got time. It's not like we're trapped here forever." He helped Jeff bring in the last of the items and set them on the living room table, while the rest of the group tended to their own needs. Vivian went to work sorting them into their proper places.

"Pardon me for asking, but is it supposed to be this chilly in here?"

"I usually leave the setting low in the winter to preserve fuel," Jeff said. "The most important thing is to keep the pipes from freezing. But I'll raise the temperature in a minute. First, I wanna go out and check the gauge."

"Thank you," Vivian said. Jeff started to turn toward the door, but stopped when he saw her smile. For a moment, he was caught in its trance. Finally, he returned the gesture with a smile of his own.

The toilet flushed and Dillon stepped out of bathroom, midway through zipping up his fly. He saw his girl and host in the middle of their brief exchange, which broke after a moment as Jeff went out the door. Vivian's smile disappeared immediately after seeing him.

In months prior, she could at least pretend to be happy to see him. It was easy enough to fake a smile. At least, it was back then. Now, she couldn't hide her feelings of discontent. After the year of name-calling, forced sexual situations, and striking followed by fake apologies, she had finally had enough. Not only that, she was tired of the bar fights, bailing him out of jail, catching him cheating, and now turning her into a criminal on the run.

"Everything good?" he asked, faking concern. His act was so stale, she couldn't help but chuckle.

"Dandy," she lied.

Jeff cupped a hand over his eyes as he made his way to the propane tank. He moved to the back and checked the gauge.

"What the hell?" he said to himself. The gauge showed it was less than a quarter-full. "Those sons of bitches!" He tapped on it to make sure it wasn't frozen or otherwise broken. The needle remained in the same position.

He took a deep breath. Normally, this wouldn't present a huge problem, even in this weather. He could keep the thermostat down, as long as it remained above freezing. Jeff was more than accustomed to living in low temperatures. Hell, after Afghanistan, he actually relished the cold sometimes. As long as the water pipes didn't freeze, he would easily keep the fireplace going and be comfortable.

The concern came from how his companions would react; Dillon in particular. The prick would probably use this as an excuse to hold back the rest of his payment. The thought reminded Jeff of his concerns with Dillon and his violent behavior.

Fuck, why did I agree to this?

The weightlessness of his wallet answered his question. He needed money, and they offered him thirty-grand for simply staying in his cabin for two weeks. It sounded like a simple matter at the time. But now...

Jeff went to the SUV and pulled his Smith and Wesson Model 10 revolver from under his seat. He checked the cylinders then holstered it under his coat, then hurried back to the cabin.

Vivian tensed as Dillon closed the distance between them. She could see his muscles bulging under that black sweater. His face was red, with a spot of purple near the busted vein under his scar.

"You're starting to get on my last nerve, girl," he said in a low, threatening tone.

Vivian took a breath. Her heart was starting to race again. The shakes were gradually returning. Yet, she forced herself to stand firm.

"Not hard to do," she replied, her voice shaky. She awaited his inevitable angry outburst. His knuckles cracked as his fist tightened.

"Vivian, I am close to—"

"To what?" she said. Dillon cocked his head, his mouth agape in displeasure. She dared to challenge *him?* His jaw tightened, his veins now bulging. She really needed to be taught a lesson. And he would see to it that she paid up.

The door flung open. Dillon glanced over his shoulder and saw Jeff step in. He disguised a groan as a cough, then walked to the thermostat.

"How do I turn the heat up?" he asked, eyeballing the device. Without waiting for a response, he started reaching for a knob on the side.

"You're not," Jeff said.

"The hell I'm not," Dillon barked.

"Unless you wanna sleep outside," Jeff warned. "Raise that thing, then it won't be too long until we're at that point." Dillon shot him a look.

"You said you filled the propane tank," he said. The exchange drew the attention of Keith and Matt, who came down the stairs. The latter, of course, was in the middle of filling his flask with bourbon.

"What's going on?" Keith asked.

Jeff let out a strong exhale.

"I guess the propane company wasn't able to make it in time," he said.

"The hell are you talking about?" Dillon snapped. "You said you'd have this place prepped and ready. We paid you to—"

"You've paid me hardly anything," Jeff said. He noticed the others looking visibly concerned. To each of them, it suddenly felt a lot colder in the cabin.

"So, what do we do?" Keith asked.

"I've got to keep the heat to a minimum to preserve the fuel," Jeff said. "Probably be best to keep most of the lights off as well. Run as little electricity as possible. I have lanterns and candles available, and we have a little bit of firewood to heat the place up."

"That's comforting," Dillon groaned. "Might as well live in the eighteenth century."

"Not even close to being that bad," Jeff said. "Besides, after this weather let's up, they'll probably be in. We just need to get through the next couple of days."

"We have enough blankets for the time being," Keith said. "We'll survive."

"It's coming out of his paycheck, though," Dillon said.

"Whatever," Jeff said. He went to the fireplace and knelt to stuff it with crumpled newspaper and wood. He struck a match and started the fire, stuffing a couple more balls of paper to keep the heat up until the logs finally caught flame. He then inspected the stack of wood he had handy. It would only be enough to get them into the evening. "Looks like I have more work to do."

"What do you mean?" Vivian asked.

"To keep the place heated, the fire will have to be maintained through the night. We don't have enough firewood in here to last us that long. I know where there's some logs. There's a spot down near the lake where a tree fell a long time ago. It's been cut into sections that need to be split. Going there and back will be a pain in the ass in this weather, but it beats freezing our asses off."

"Even less prepared," Dillon remarked, just loud enough to be heard. Jeff resisted the urge to respond. He could already feel the heat between them starting to escalate out of control.

"You need help?" Keith asked.

"It would make it go quicker," Jeff said. "I have two axes out in the shed."

Dillon put a hand on Matt's shoulder and goaded him toward the door.

"You go too," he said.

"Why me?" Matt complained.

"Because I want this taken care of quickly," he said. Vivian stepped back toward the fireplace. It was a lie he just told. He just wanted privacy to do God knows what.

"Yeah, no thanks," Matt said. "They said it themselves, they only have two axes."

Jeff glared at him. At this point, he didn't trust Dillon at all. And the way he was looking at Vivian was like a lion looking at fresh meat. The thought of leaving him alone with Vivian did not sit well.

"Matt, how drunk are you?"

"I'm not drunk?" Matt answered.

"You said it like you're asking a question."

"Oh! Did I?"

"Why don't I go with you?" Vivian asked. Jeff glanced to her. The thought was actually a smart one.

"You good with that?" he asked.

"Absolutely!" Vivian responded enthusiastically. "I can handle an axe." Jeff nodded, trying to hold back a grin after seeing the subtle twitches in Dillon's expression.

"Okay, we'll leave in five," he said.

Dillon simply walked back into his room, pretending to be unfazed by the exchange that had just taken place. He laid in the bed and pretended to lose himself in a novel, while in actuality, he watched out the corner of his eye as Vivian and Jeff bundled up together.

He noticed the change in her demeanor. She *liked* being with this Jeff guy. And despite his efforts to seem indifferent, he liked her. Dillon's jaw tightened. He wouldn't allow anyone to steal anything from him. Least of all his girl. His hands squeezed the book, crumpling it as though wrapping his hands around Jeff's throat. It was a sensation he would love to see realized.

CHAPTER 9

Deputy Rick Beck blasted the heat to its max, trying to warm the SUV's windshield as best as he could. Snow melted into beads of water that streaked all over the windshield, which would then freeze in the wind, appearing like crystal veins.

"They should pay us double-time for being out in this shit," his partner, Simon Mayer, complained. Simon sipped on his coffee, watching the snow assault the vehicle as they slowly patrolled the road.

"I could use it," Rick Beck said.

"Why?" Simon chuckled. "You'd just invest it. Part of your holy crusade to retire early."

"That's the idea," Rick replied. He hated this routine of patrolling the same streets over and over again. He hated it even more so in the winter. At forty-years old, he had done it a million times over, in three different counties. To sum it up, he was bored. And unfortunately, he saw no other way out of this life other than retirement.

He wore the watch he had during his days as a detective in Louisville. With one of the highest crime rates in the country, Rick was an everyday *Dick Tracy*. There was never a shortage of cases to be solved. He made a name for himself, putting criminals away one after another, with enough evidence for the prosecutor to pull out an easy win.

Things took a turn when he investigated a judge whom he believed to be receiving payments from a mobster. Soon, his cases were dismissed, and his suspects were released without explanation, despite evidence presented. To make matters worse, the media presented Rick as a maverick cop who overstepped his bounds with the law.

He tightened his grip on the steering wheel as the memories tortured his brain.

The District Attorney and Chief of Police had ignored his concerns. As time went on, they became more concerned with their public image rather than enforcing the law. Despite pushback, Rick continued the case, digging into financial records while pushing the local mob's money laundering scheme. This inevitably led to a confrontation, which escalated quickly into a fist fight followed by a brief shootout. Rick had taken a bullet in his left forearm for his efforts. That scar paled to the media coverage that followed. He was shunned by his own department for supposedly exceeding his boundaries, and was fired by the department within a week.

The termination came with blacklisting. No city department wanted his name on their payroll. Only the Blessing County Sheriff's Department was willing to overlook his 'mistakes' of the past. Blessing County was a small stretch of country with a few good communities... and Ellisville, which rested on the northwest corner. They hardly patrolled that area, and half of the calls received from there turned out to be wild goose chases. Only Rick was bored enough to even respond to those calls.

Simon let out a sigh as they passed the sign *Welcome to Ellisville.* The top of the rectangular sign was half bent, the only word readable being Ellisville. Old Steve, the clerk at that station, had phoned Dispatch at least five times before they decided to send their vehicle on the call. It wasn't uncommon for him to phone the department. Though they were never prank calls, they were usually miniscule problems that amounted to nothing.

"You sure we even want to waste our time with this?" Simon said.

"You got something better to do?" Rick asked. Simon shrugged his shoulders.

"Well, maybe. Sure!"

"Yeah? What?"

"Plenty of things," Simon said.

"Yeah? Like stopping at Miss Rucker's place to 'investigate suspicious activity'?"

Simon looked to the window, resisting the urge to let his devious grin show.

"Well..." the smile finally showed, "Janet has many concerns."

"Yeah, I'm sure," Rick said. "I'm sure her heating system isn't part of those concerns."

"It can get cold this time of year," Simon joked. "She needs someone to help her, you know...feel warm..."

"Okay, alright! That's enough," Rick said, shaking his head. "I do NOT know why I pursued that topic. Ugh!"

"'Cause you're jealous, maybe?" Simon said, chuckling.

"Of you and Janet Rucker? I wouldn't parade that a great triumph. She's been kinda known for getting around."

"Not lately, not since hooking up with me!" Simon said. Rick shook his head, trying to get the images out of his mind's eye. His efforts only increased his buddy's enjoyment. "What can I say? You know the deal: Once you go black, you can never go back!"

"Oh, Jesus," Rick muttered.

It was such a small county with small towns. Nothing ever happened, and the sheriff knew it. From what Rick could tell in his four years as a Blessing County Sheriff's Deputy, the sheriff simply expected his people to clock in, patrol, and clock out. Maybe respond to a call or two. Beyond that, whatever happened in-between, as long as it wasn't illegal, was fair game. Good for someone who was just coasting through life. Bad for someone like Rick, whose mind needed something constructive to do.

The roads here had not been plowed, forcing Rick to drive through eight inches of snow. He engaged the four-wheel drive and continued on through, inching his way until he could see the intersection up ahead near Willie's Gas Station.

"Look who's decided to join us," Simon said. Rick looked at his rearview mirror. It took a moment for the back windshield wiper to clear off enough of a view for him to see. He saw the snow-covered hood of a police Chevy Colorado trailing a hundred yards behind them. Only one person they knew drove that truck.

"Wow," Rick said. "I guess Eddie's bored as well."

"REALLY bored," Simon said. "That, or he's looking for an excuse to be off the road for a few minutes."

Rick was secretly grateful. Though he was friends with Simon, Eddie was the one person on the unit that openly expressed a desire to move on to bigger and better things. Despite the few calls dealt with by this department, Eddie was also one of the few that displayed a good work ethic. His uniform was always pressed, as opposed to the shaky, wrinkled shirts worn by some of the other deputies. The three of them had sparked a friendship, and would get together for grill-outs and movies. And while on the same shift, they'd share calls. Not that there was much else to do.

"Maybe." Rick approached the intersection and pulled into the gas station's driveway. He nearly got stuck twice doing so. He pulled his winter hat down over his head and opened the door. The wind attempted to carry him off right away. Snow bunched at his shins as he waited for his partner to step out of the passenger side.

The wind blew off his hat, exposing his bald head. He reached back to catch it, but missed.

"Damn it!" he cursed. "I want July. I want fishing. I want grass. I want to complain about mowing again." The truck pulled up behind him and parked. Deputy Eddie Moore stepped out, grinning ear-to-ear.

"Lose something there, Simon?"

"Oh, shut up!"

They quickly approached the door. It swung wide. In the open path stood the scrawny, crooked-necked Steve.

"Come in! Come in!" he said, waving them over enthusiastically. "Let me serve you fine officers some coffee."

"Nahhh, that's quite alright," all three of them replied simultaneously.

"Suit yourself!" Steve said.

"Let's get to it, Steve," Rick said. "What's going on? Why are you blowing up our phone lines?"

"Because I saw the ones!" he said excitedly.

"The ones?" Eddie said, his face wrinkling. Already, the thirty-four-year-old deputy regretted accompanying his buddies to this call.

"Yes. I have seen the mark! The guilty ones have passed through! And they will see judgement for their heinous crimes!"

The three cops shared a glance.

"Okay…Steve…if you don't quit with this apocalyptic talk, I'm going to beat you over the head with a bible," Rick said.

"Who are you reporting?" Simon added.

"The murderers from Richardson!" Steve said. "They've been here!"

"Beg your pardon?" Eddie said.

"Haven't you seen the news?" Steve was finally speaking like a normal person. "The bank robbery this morning that left two people dead."

"Wait, *them*?"

"The ones who killed the cop?" Simon asked. Even his eyes lit up. The news of the killing had spread across the state like wildfire. Each department had been provided the limited information that the Richardson detectives could muster. "You saw them? You sure? When?"

"Oh, early this afternoon," Steve said.

"How do you know it was them?" Rick asked.

"I had some people come in that I've never seen before," Old Steve answered. "One of them was a woman. She had a tattoo on her right wrist. It was the same tattoo that they showed on the news."

Rick pulled his I-phone and brought up the saved image of the shark tattoo, then showed it to Steve.

"This one?"

"YES!" Steve said. "That was the one."

"How many were in their group?" Eddie asked.

"I don't know. At least three," Steve said. "I didn't get a good enough look. I didn't realize they were the killers at first."

"We don't know that now," Eddie said.

"You have security cameras?" Rick said.

"None   that   work."
"Figures," Eddie said.

"Which way did they go?" Rick asked. Old Steve pointed down the road. Simon and Eddie were both shaking their heads.

Wild goose chase, Simon mouthed. Eddie nodded subtly in agreement. Rick, on the other hand, was watching the road. There was nothing but country out in that direction, with the only intersection being Line Street.

"Thanks, Steve. We'll take it from here," he said.

"Not a problem, officers." Steve started back for his checkout counter. "Sure I can't serve you up some hot joe?" All three cops glanced at the coffee machine and the dark brown globs that had dripped over the sides.

"Nah, no thank you," each of them said. Steve grinned and continued to his counter while the cops gathered by the entrance. Simon was glaring at his patrol partner and shaking his head.

"I know what you're thinking, Rick," he said. "I'm telling you, it's a wild goose chase. The guy probably saw the tattoo, then saw the people, and in his crazed mind, he linked the two together."

"That's probably not far from the truth," Eddie said. Rick was silent for a minute, listening to the howl of the wind as he thought about the information.

"If I was a cold-blooded criminal, and had just committed a crime and didn't want to be found, what would I do?" he said. Simon bit his lip and hung his head in frustration. "I'd want to find a place to lay low for a while, long enough for the heat to blow over. If there's no trace, then eventually it'll be easier to use that stolen money without anyone growing suspicious."

"I doubt they're hiding out here in Ellisville," Simon said.

"No, but maybe they went somewhere else," Rick said. He looked to the southwest at the elevation of land and forest. Beyond that was a large lake where hardly anyone ever visited. Eddie read his mind.

"You're not seriously suggesting they went all the way up to Circle Mountain?" he asked.

"It'd be a perfect place to hide, provided they have enough electricity," Rick said.

"That's awfully thin, Mr. Detective," Simon said. "The Sheriff's not gonna go for it."

Rick thought about it for another minute, then checked his watch. 4:30. The sheriff would be leaving his office at 5:00. Rick pulled out his phone and dialed his personal cell phone.

****

Sheriff Warren J. Glynn closed the windows on his computer and started packing up his things. With the weather so bad, he decided he'd get an early start out the door. There was nothing left for him to do anyway. Monday was 'administration day' where he worked on payroll, hours, and scheduled a few meetings. The Blessing County Sheriff's Department had little in the way of any HR staff. In fact, all they had were six dispatchers, twenty-four deputy sheriffs, a few reserves who often never reported for duty, and a few office staff. It wasn't much for a sheriff to manage, which was one of the reasons he took this job.

His badges from former areas of service were preserved on his shelf. The first was his State Trooper badge, where he served for twenty years before retiring at the age of forty-one. He couldn't imagine going back to the fast-paced life of a trooper. The mandated overtime, long patrols, irritable co-workers, and of course, the public. The next two badges were from two separate universities he worked on. But neither of those jobs lasted long. Dealing with obnoxious twenty-somethings all day made him lose faith in the younger generation. At least here in Blessing County, there was some trace of decency. At least, he made himself think that was the case. It was enough for him to coast by, which showed in his increasingly expanding waistline. It was a stark contrast from the fit man who graduated from the Kentucky State Trooper academy of '89.

He felt his phone vibrate against his waist. He looked at the screen, then groaned after recognizing the number.

"Not him again," he said. Ever since Rick got hired, he was always trying to be the maverick detective he was back in Louisville. Every little case the department got, Rick Beck would make a mountain out of a molehill. And here he was doing it again. Warren was tempted not to answer the call.

Gotta do it, that voice in his mind said. He held the phone to his ear. "Yeah?"

"Sheriff. It's Rick. Hey, we might have a lead on those bank robbers from Richardson."

For a moment, Warren's interest was piqued.

"Yeah? What makes you say that?"

"We've spoken to a witness that claims they've seen the tattoo that's been reported by Richardson PD. It was on a female, like the reports indicated."

"Anyone could have a tattoo," Warren said.

"Yeah, but Sheriff, the person was in a group. I think they've gone to one of the cabins at Lake Shadow to wait out the manhunt."

Warren shook his head. There was nothing to back that claim up. The problem with this entire scenario was the insufficient evidence. That, and there was no way in hell he would trek all the way down to Lake Shadow on a hunch.

"And where'd this information come from?"

"Well..." there was a pause. Warren heard a sigh, indicating Rick was reluctant to admit something. *"Old Steve from the gas station."*

Warren wanted to hang up right there.

"Rick...I'm gonna try and be nice. I think you were a good cop in Louisville. I do think you got a raw deal. Hence, I hired you when nobody else would. Do me a favor; quit trying to be a detective again."

"Sir, I'll volunteer to go out there myself and check it out."

"Hell no," Warren said. "Not in this weather. Not with an hour of daylight left. I'm not authorizing it, Beck. Alright? I gotta go."

****

Simon watched as Rick lowered his phone in defeat.

"I take it that went well."

Rick checked the time again. The sheriff did have one good point; it would be foolish to head all the way out there this late in the day. Especially in this weather.

"I think I'm gonna try to get some overtime. Morning shift tomorrow morning perhaps," he said. Both deputies glared at him.

"Beg your pardon?" Simon said.

"In the morning, I'm gonna take one of the snowmobiles out there. It'll be easier than using a truck. I just want to check the area out."

"Hmm..." Eddie said. "You want company?"

"You even capable of waking up before ten in the morning?" Rick asked.

"Of course," Eddie said.

"Ohhhhh, you guys are insane," Simon said.

"Hey, nobody said you had to come," Rick said.

"Good. I don't plan to," Simon said. "You guys have fun. Go ahead and try to recapture your former glory. Maybe you'll earn yourself another medallion for valor. Still got your old one in your shirt pocket?" Rick didn't answer. Simon smiled. "You do, don't ya? Eddie, have you seen it?" Eddie shook his head. "Go ahead. Whip it out."

Rick looked over at Eddie. The young officer was visibly curious. He had often expressed interest in Rick's background, seeking inspiration to move on to a brighter career beyond Blessing County. Rick reached into his shirt pocket and found the gold medallion. Attached to it was a blue stripe. He could see the inspiration in the impressionable deputy's face.

"You know, you ought to frame that," Simon said. "What? You take it everywhere you go? You sleep with it at night?"

Eddie glanced at Simon.

"Speaking of sleep: Sleep in tomorrow, why don't ya? Have some hot cocoa before another audacious tour of duty on the afternoon shift. We'll actually do some police work."

"Let him," Rick said. He tucked the medal back into his pocket. "You and I can handle the trip. He'd probably slow us down anyway." He and Eddie chuckled.

"Yeah. Shit! That brings to mind the last time we all went snowmobiling. How long did it take for us to dig him out of that snowbank?"

Simon grimaced. He was feeling the police version of peer pressure crushing down on him. He glanced out the window. He for one didn't mind the routine. It suited him. But the more he thought about it, he decided it'd be nice to have one good police story under his belt. If nothing else, it would break the mould.

"Fine." He pointed at Rick. "You're getting the Starbucks!"

CHAPTER 10

Dillon sat up from the bed the minute the door shut behind Jeff and Vivian. He stepped into the living room, seeing snow swirling over the furniture. Keith was seated on the couch, glaring back at him.

"Matt!" Dillon called, ignoring Keith. He listened to the drunkard's stumbling footsteps as he made his way down the stairs.

"What's up, Boss?" he said, pinching his flask tight.

"I need you to bundle up and follow those two," Dillon said.

"What? Why?" Matt complained.

"I don't trust that guy," Dillon answered. "I don't want him taking anything but the money we paid him."

"You think he's gonna make a move on your girl?" Matt chuckled as the question came out. He lifted his flask to his lips, then squealed when he felt Dillon's fingers closing around his collar. Next thing he knew, his feet were dangling an inch off the floor. Matt swallowed. "You know? That would be foolish of him!"

"Yes, it would," Dillon growled. He let go. Matt immediately scurried for his coat.

Keith stood up from his chair. "Good God, Dillon."

"You have a problem?"

"It's five degrees out," Keith said. "What? You think they're gonna do it in the snow?"

"I want an eye kept on him," Dillon repeated.

"We're in *his* cabin," Keith said. "This would be a clean break if you didn't shoot the manager and the cop!"

"Vivian fucked it up," Dillon said. "If she did her job properly and kept an eye on that banker, he wouldn't have hit the alarm."

56

"And shooting him changed nothing," Keith said. "Except up the price on our heads. Then of course, you shot the cop."

"He shot first."

"No, *you* did. And now, every cop across the state is looking for us."

"You knew the risks when you joined me on this," Dillon said. "You were there at the bank. You crossed the fence. I don't see you turning yourself in." Keith exhaled slowly through his nostrils. Whether he liked it or not, Dillon made an accurate point. And judging by the way the bastard was smiling, he knew he'd won the argument. "Why don't you go count your cash? And call the buyers for the jewelry."

"There's no service out here," Keith reminded him.

"Oh…right," Dillon said. He watched Matt approach the door, chugging at his flask the whole way. Something was bothering him. The guy appeared to be particularly anxious. He hugged his overcoat and opened the wooden door, then stared at the array of trees swaying in the distance. "What the hell's the problem? Afraid the boogieman's waiting for you out there?"

Matt looked back at him, his eyes expressing a genuine sense of dread. In return, he received a hellish stare from the group leader. Suddenly, Matt felt himself warming up from the winter cold already. He grinded his teeth together, reminding himself that *thing* he saw was just his mind playing tricks on him.

But then again…what killed that deer? He shrugged. Any cougar could have gotten that deer. *Yeah, that's what it was.* It helped a little to relax his nerves. However, what haunted him in his imagination paled to the intensifying body language exhibited by Dillon. Matt unlatched the screen door. He only had it open a crack before the wind grabbed hold of it, flinging it out the rest of the way. In frantic, disorderly motions, Matt pressed the door shut and started following the tracks left by Vivian and Jeff.

Dillon shook his head and shut the main door.

"Pathetic," he mumbled. "And drunk." Keith seethed as Dillon stepped back into his bedroom.

And yet, you're making him go out there.

Thick snowflakes flew through the air like little white bullets, assaulting every inch of Matt's body as he stumbled through the front yard. The wind was blinding, forcing him to keep a hand over his face.

There were two sets of tracks leading down to the lake. Matt kept going, keeping his eyes on the ground directly below him. Already, he was longing for the warmth of the fire. Hell, just to be out of the wind would suffice. He kept his face covered as he continued following the trail. The sun was less than an hour away from setting, which gave the grey sky a darker tinge. If not for the icy precipitation, he would've guessed they were under an intense thunderstorm.

Still walking as he stared up into the sky, Matt was unaware that he was on the ledge of a hill that led to the lake. The slight drop in elevation was enough to cause the drunkard to lose his balance. He threw his arms out and pedaled his legs, trying to keep upright. The effort only resulted in a more flamboyant fall. He hit the snow and rolled over his shoulder. The tumble led him several meters down, nearly putting his face into the foot of a tree.

Matt spat snow as he lifted his head from the ground. He quickly stood back to his feet and straightened his hood. He took a step back, only to trip over a rock and fall again. He sat up, his coat smothered in powder.

"God, it's been forever since I had a drink," he mumbled. He reached into his coat pocket, his fingers searching for his flask. However, they found nothing but lint. It wasn't there. Matt's eyes went wide. In an instant, he was on his hands and knees digging for the object. His hands swept through snow as though trying to splash it.

A slight glint caught his eye. Leaning up on his knees, he looked out, seeing the top half of the flask exposed from the snow. He sprinted the few feet between it and him. He already had the top halfway screwed open before he even lifted it from the snow.

The alcohol was like heaven on his lips, though his stomach experienced a rather dull feeling from the ulcers he was starting to develop. But Matt didn't care. He lowered the flask and contemplated draining the rest of it. In that moment, he had nearly forgotten why he was even out here. He glanced at the snow and trees. Suddenly, his brain registered the icy touch of the wind again.

What was I doing? I—uh...

"Oh, shit!" he said. He looked back and forth in search of the tracks. He had lost the trail after his stupid stumble. He instead searched for his own trail, hoping to find his way back.

He found a small trench in the snow. That had to have been the trail he made when he fell. Without hesitating, Matt followed the line in the snow. He walked for several minutes, then realized he wasn't going uphill. Yet, the trail continued.

It HAD to be his trail. After all, there was nothing else that fell in the snow...

A memory flash brought him to a stop. He gave the trench a closer look, then stepped back. There were enormous tracks beside it. They were like a man's only much larger. And the shape... it was as though each footprint had a set of horns. He stood straight, continuing to study the trail. The way the tracks, if they were tracks, and the trench were set up, it made him think of somebody walking in the snow while dragging something heavy.

His mind flashed to the dead deer he saw before...and the thing in the woods.

"It was just a tree," he reminded himself. "Just a short, oddly shaped tree." He thought about turning around to find his way back to the cabin. Of course, he'd have to face Dillon's wrath for showing up before Jeff and Vivian. These days, Dillon was a little too trigger happy, which always had Matt feeling on edge. He would have to come up with a lie to tell Dillon. Unless he got lucky, and Vivian and Jeff somehow returned ahead of him.

A thought crossed his mind. He looked at the trail. Jeff had a large sack to carry the wood. Perhaps it was heavy and he had to drag it to bring it back. That would explain a few things...even though the sack was not that large. But Matt's intoxicated brain wasn't capable of connecting the little details. He went with his theory and followed the trail. It went along the snowed-over shoreline, then it curved out into the trees.

It was several minutes before Matt realized he should've arrived at the cabin by now. He looked to the sky again. Night was approaching, stripping away what little light he had.

Matt stopped. Up ahead was what appeared to be a rock wall that towered for nearly fifty feet. The tracks led right up to it. Matt took in a shaky breath and continued. Now, he was driven by curiosity. This was obviously not the cabin.

He weaved around a few trees and approached the large rock structure. The tracks disappeared at the mouth of a jagged opening at the base. It was almost twice as tall as him, and over three times his width. He realized he was looking at a cave.

At that moment, he noticed that there were several of these strange tracks in the snow. None were as fresh as this current trail, and many of them seemed to go to-and-fro between the cave and the assortment of trees around it.

That's when Matt noticed large lumps in the snow. Initially, he assumed they were just that: lumps of snow. Then his eyes caught little creases in the shapes. There were 'extensions' protruding from those lumps. Matt held his flask to his lips and approached the nearest one. It was lying near a tree, covered in snow. The toe of his boot bumped against something. He took a swig and swept his foot, unburying whatever it was.

First, he saw the hoof. Then the bones of the leg it was attached to. Matt swallowed as he noticed the busted ribcage and antlers. His eyes went to the cave and back to the skeleton. Now he was questioning his drinking habits. He wondered if he was really seeing these things, or if his imagination was playing tricks on him. Either way, it was enough to make him turn back.

He turned on his heel and searched for his own tracks to guide him back. His foot hit something else. There was another lump in the snow, this one a bit shallower. Whatever was buried, it was fresher than the deer. He saw the bones of a limb, the meat having been stripped away. But there was no hoof at the end of this limb. There were five digits, all curled at the knuckles. The snow dusted away, revealing the knob shape of the shoulder, and the boned chest plate. There was no head.

Beside it were the torn remains of clothing, completely shredded, flapping in the wind.

A grinding sound entered his ears. From inside the cave came the sound of something being crunched. Like rock. Or bone. Something was in that cave.

Matt squealed and ran as fast as he could, plowing face first into a tree almost immediately. He spun, miraculously finding his balance. There was movement coming from the cave. He saw a shape standing a few feet inside the opening. The same shape as he saw in the woods. And like that shape in the woods, it was staring back at him.

Matt backpedaled then turned, finally finding this own trail and followed it back to where he came.

CHAPTER 11

"Alright, this'll do," Jeff shouted over the wind at Vivian. She slammed her axe down on the last piece of log, splitting it in two. It was clear she was no stranger to the outdoors way of living. She held the axe over her shoulder while Jeff collected the two remaining pieces and stacked them in his tote. It would be enough to last through the night. Tomorrow, Jeff would come out and get more. Right now, he just wanted to get the hell out of this wind. Not only that, but his sciatica was starting to act up, firing pain signals from his back to his leg.

"Hope you can get enough electricity to make coffee," Vivian said. Jeff chuckled.

"Yes, I think we'll survive," he said. He lifted the heavy tote with one arm and followed their trail back to the cabin. His smile disappeared as he saw the porch in the distance and the orange glow from the fireplace through the window. He knew Dillon would be waiting in there, anxious to stir up another confrontation. The same dread was visible across Vivian's face as well.

To the left was the storage shed, the door flapping in the wind. They crossed the yard and stepped inside, placing the axes in the proper places.

"How dangerous is he?" Jeff asked.

"I thought you didn't want to know," Vivian said.

"I didn't because it seemed like a simple enough matter," Jeff said. "Even when we first met and arranged this deal, he seemed somewhat anxious and short-tempered, but now he seems unhinged. And dangerous. And I want to know how dangerous."

Vivian felt her throat tighten, both from dread and a flashback from him actually clutching her throat.

"He's very dangerous," she said. "You shouldn't have accepted this deal."

"I'm already regretting it," Jeff said.

"Feel guilty about helping a bunch of criminals?" Vivian asked. There was guilt in her own voice, making Jeff wonder if the question was directed at herself.

"There is a little bit of that," Jeff admitted. "But again, it seemed like a harmless enough matter. Simple bank robbery, hideout, then disappear. But now…"

"You wonder if he's gonna tie up another loose end," Vivian completed his sentence.

"That neighborhood was flooding with cops," Jeff said. "Even for a five-eleven, they don't work that fast. Unless something REALLY drastic occurred." Vivian was looking at the ground. She worried that Dillon would somehow figure out she told Jeff these things. "He shot somebody, didn't he?" Vivian gave a shaky nod.

"The banker and a cop," she said.

"Oh, Christ," Jeff said. A sharp exhale exploded into a warm cloud that scattered in the wind. "What was I thinking, getting involved in this?"

"Believe me, I ask myself the same question," Vivian said. She looked at Jeff. He had stopped, staring off at the cabin despite the wind and snow. It was no longer a 'harmless robbery', not that such a thing ever existed. But it was enough that Jeff could live with it. But now, the game had changed. "What are you gonna do?"

"Right now? I'm gonna get this wood up to the cabin and have some of that coffee you're eager to make," he said. "Tomorrow, I'm gonna cut up that tree. Then…I'll wait until nightfall. Sneak out while they're asleep and alert law enforcement."

"Won't that get you in trouble?" she asked.

"Maybe," Jeff said. "All I can do is hope that blowing the whistle will get me off with a light punishment."

"Dillon's a light sleeper," Vivian said. "He'll hear you start the engine."

"Not if we crumple some pills into his dinner or coffee," Jeff said. "I've got some stuff that'll have him sleeping like a baby. He'll never know I left."

"You have pills?"

"Sleeping pills. Melatonin," Jeff said. Vivian stepped close to him.

"Take me with you," she said. Jeff looked at her. "Please."

"You were never meant for this life of crime, were you?"

"No," Vivian said. "I hate it. I can't stand constantly looking over my shoulder. Now it's worse than ever. Plus being with Dillon is pure agony. I've wanted to leave, but he'd threaten me. Then, I saw him murder... I just want to start over."

Jeff nodded. The girl was telling the truth.

"Okay," he said. "You'll have to tell them everything about these guys. They'll arrest you too, you know?"

"I know," she said. "Can't be worse than living with him. What about you? You were doing this because you needed money."

The howl of the wind was no match for Jeff's groan.

"I guess I'll have to toss aside my pride and get a job at Walmart," he said. "Or go back to school. Settle for the dull life."

"I'll choose that dull life anytime," Vivian said. She leaned in close and planted her lips to his. Jeff was surprised, yet didn't make any move to stop her. Finally, they separated.

"You've known me for less than twenty-four hours, but you want to run off with me?"

"Compared to what I've been stuck with all my life?" Vivian said. "You're the first man I've come across with any sense of decency. I've seen more honor in you in the last *twenty-four* hours than all the years with Dillon."

Jeff didn't challenge her point. Looking at it from her perspective, it made enough sense. Jeff wasn't typically one to ride off into the sunset with a girl he hardly knew, but then again, past relationships that formed under 'normal' circumstances never fared so well. One cheated while he was overseas, another left him in favor of focusing on her career.

"Let's start over together," Vivian said.

"Oh, what the hell?" Jeff said. They shared another kiss.

A strange noise from outside caused them to separate. They could hear frantic breathing as well as running feet. Jeff reached under his coat and clutched his revolver, thinking perhaps Dillon had stepped out and saw their interaction. But there was no movement around the front of the cabin. It wasn't Dillon or Keith.

They stepped out of the shed. There was a figure parading through the snow.

"Matt?" Vivian asked.

His eyes were wide, hot breath trailing rapidly from his mouth like from a steam engine. He was moving at a brisk pace, even in the thick snow, as though the devil was right behind him.

"Whoa, fella," Jeff said. He grabbed Matt by the shoulders and stopped him. "What the hell were you doing? You could've ended up in the lake!" Matt didn't respond. Even through the thick coat, Jeff could feel his rapid heartbeat.

"I—I, uh," Matt stammered. The front door opened. Dillon peeked outside, glaring at him with tense eyes. "I had to take a piss. Keith was hogging up the bathroom, if you know what I mean."

Jeff looked over his shoulder at Dillon.

"Yeah, I do," he said. All three of them went back into the cabin. Jeff took Vivian's coat and went to the closet, while she stepped into the kitchen to make coffee.

"How the hell'd you get all the way over there?" Dillon whispered to Matt. He didn't answer. He stared out the window with a blank expression, like a mental patient. He chugged the remaining contents from his flask. Dillon resisted the urge to grab him by the shoulders. "What? You see a ghost or something?"

Matt coughed and shook his head.

"No." His voice trembled.

"Then what's the problem?"

"I thought I saw something," Matt said.

"*Saw something*? What do you mean you saw something? Saw what?" Dillon pried the flask out of Matt's hands. "Yeah, I'm sure you *saw* something. You probably saw flying saucers and little green men. You need to cut this shit out." Matt flung his hands for the flask, only to trip and faceplant on the wooden floor. "Case and point."

"Whoa?!" Jeff exclaimed. He and Keith quickly approached the two.

"Dillon, leave him alone," Vivian said. Dillon's glare locked onto her. He didn't know where this newfound disobedience came from, but he would get to the bottom of it. He then looked back at the men, a subtle twitch giving away his surprise at the holstered revolver on Jeff's belt. Dillon's first instinct was to question him about it, but he already knew the answer. It was a deliberate show of power.

Keith helped Matt to his feet and guided him up the stairs to his room. Jeff proceeded to the fireplace and stocked the woodpile. As he did, he found himself glancing over at Vivian. She had filled a filter with coffee grounds and poured the water. The new memory of their kiss flooded his mind. He still felt the sensation on his lips. It was a joyous feeling that he didn't want to go away.

Dillon's presence became all the more ominous in that moment. Jeff watched him in his peripheral vision. He had stepped back into his room, like a Neanderthal in his cave.

"I'll get started on dinner," Jeff said.

CHAPTER 12

Vivian rocked in the living room chair and watched the flames dance within the fireplace. She placed her empty plate on a nearby tray table and wrapped her blanket over her shoulders. The orange glow of the fire was the main source of light inside the cabin at the moment. The lights were turned off, except for a couple of lanterns and a few mint-flavored candles scattered about.

Shadows danced along the living room floor as the flames twisted, the wood beneath them cracking. Her eyes went to the window. Aside from the flickering glow, it was a black screen. Tiny white blobs peppered the other side and fell off as the storm continued to punish the cabin.

The floor creaked behind her. Vivian didn't bother looking. It was Dillon doing a second set of pushups. He had to have hit his one-hundred count by now and was aiming to do a second set. Vivian didn't watch; she could hardly stand to look at him.

Dishes clanked together in the kitchen sink as soapy water swirled around them. Vivian watched the kitchen in the corner of her eye, specifically Jeff as he cleaned up the place. The countertops and dining room table were scrubbed, and everyone's dinner plates had been collected. The guy was a decent host, even for a pack of criminals.

She wanted to join him in there, just to be close to him. But she couldn't make her new affections too obvious. She had to play things normally for at least another day.

"I'm going upstairs," Dillon said. Vivian kept her eyes on the dishes.

"Okay."

"You need anything from up there?" he asked. Vivian's stomach tightened. Every so often he pretended to be nice. She'd fallen for that act before. It was all part of the emotional manipulation, not only so she would be afraid to leave, but to feel guilty about doing it. She sometimes suspected that Dillon knew she wanted out. Then again, that would require a degree of empathy, and Dillon wasn't the type to think of anyone beyond himself.

"What would I need from upstairs?" she asked. *Damn it! That's not playing it normal.*

Dillon's already tight muscles tensed further.

"Just trying to be nice," he forced himself to say.

"Thank you," she forced herself, the word 'thank' replacing another word she wanted to use. "I'm good." She hoped it would be enough to get him to go away. Her blanket disguised her cringe as he approached instead. He knelt down and folded both arms over the left armrest. He then rested his chin on them and looked at her like a lost puppy.

"What's wrong, babe?" he said.

"Nothing's wrong," she said.

Jeff watched in the corner of his eye. He'd seen the nice-guy act from people like Dillon too. It never amounted to anything good.

"You sure?" Dillon asked, his voice low-pitched and drawn out, as though trying to sound sympathetic.

"I'm sure," Vivian said. "I'm just tired. It's been a very long day."

"I hear that," he said. He turned and tilted his head toward the open bedroom door. "Well...I got the bed nice and made up."

"Thanks," she lied. "I'm just gonna hang out here."

"You're tense," he grinned, running a finger along her neck. "I know something that can help with that." Now, Vivian was visibly disgusted. The guy was completely unfazed by the things he had done earlier. Not only did it disgust her, but it terrified her as well. Someone that unaffected by such an act had likely experienced it prior in his life.

"No," she said. She leaned away as Dillon brought his lips toward her neck.

"Hey," he chuckled.

"I thought you were going upstairs," she said.

"I changed my mind," he said, wearing a wide smile across his face. He leaned in further to close the gap. Vivian was now all the way onto the other armrest. She looked over at Jeff, worried he'd be put off of her affections. Dillon started kissing her neck, working his way up to her jawline. His fingers curled under her shirt collar and slowly peeled it down.

"No," she said. Dillon chuckled.

"What?" He looked up and saw Jeff in the kitchen. His grin only grew larger. "You don't like being watched. I can take care of that." He looked back to Jeff. "Hey, dishwasher! Take a hike!"

Jeff pierced him with a stare. Dillon was already working on undoing her shirt buttons, despite Vivian's protesting body language.

"No shenanigans under this roof," Jeff said. Dillon perked up.

"What are you? Her dad?"

"Her dad would've shot you already," Jeff replied.

"Ha! Too bad he died of a heart attack already," Dillon chuckled. Vivian stood up, unwinding her blanket and walked away. Like a homing missile, Dillon followed her, cornering her near the door.

"Dillon," her voice was firm, "No. It's not happening."

"I think it is," he said. Vivian pressed her back to the door. Every effort to evade was spurring him further.

"What about him?" she asked, hoping that reminding Dillon of Jeff's presence would put him off. He only leaned in closer.

"I guess he'll have to watch. Perhaps he'll learn a thing or two." He pressed in again, only to withdraw from the sound of approaching feet. Jeff was halfway across the living room, heading directly toward him. There was a fury in his eyes that Dillon immediately registered.

The two men squared up.

"I'll say this *once*," Jeff said. "You're a guest here. I will not tolerate this kind of behavior under my roof."

"I'm paying you a hefty fee," Dillon said.

"Which I haven't received, by the way," Jeff retorted.

"Is that what's bothering you?" Dillon growled. "You'll get it. Don't worry. Now, if you don't mind…" he started to turn to continue his crusade on Vivian. A grab on his shoulder pulled him backward.

Dillon clenched his teeth in anger. He spun on his heel and swung his arm back, missing Jeff's nose by an inch.

There was a tense silence in the room. The two figures stood in the dark, each waiting for the other to make a move.

Vivian cupped her hands over her mouth, her heart pounding as she watched the light flickering over the two figures. Hands were clenched to fists. Faces were tense, like two gladiators ready to be unleashed. Yet, there was that thin thread of self-control. For Jeff, he was simply trying to control the situation. Dillon, on the other hand, knew of Jeff's revolver. The only reason he didn't advance was inner cowardice. She prayed he wouldn't find his courage. Despite being deranged, Dillon was a good shot and a fast draw, as the officer at the bank unfortunately found out.

A dull sound flooded the silence. It was deep and throaty, not coming from either of the men. Both of them, still facing each other, started glancing about the room. They heard it too.

"Matt! You need to lay off the booze!" Dillon called out.

"I don't think that's him," Jeff said. Footsteps pounded the upstairs floor as Keith and Matt approached the stairs.

"What's going on?" Keith said, noticing the two in their standoff. He then heard the sound. It was like a muffled moan combined with a growl. It wasn't like a canine. No, something bigger.

Matt remained on the top step, his hands tightening their grip on the rail.

Now there was the sound of pointed objects scraping on the wooden deck. Dillon and Jeff now completely abandoned their dispute and went to the door together. Vivian stepped aside, making way for them. Jeff grasped the door handle with one hand, his revolver with the other, then opened it a crack.

At that moment, something hit the screen door hard, causing everyone to jump back. The screen tore and the lower glass panel shattered.

"Jesus!" Dillon yelled. The whole group jumped back. Upstairs, Matt scampered out of sight, hurrying to his collection of booze.

There was another series of scraping on the deck, followed by a pounding sound against the stairs as though something was tumbling off. That dull, growly moan hummed again. Jeff returned to the door and opened it the rest of the way. He, Dillon, and Keith stepped outside through the busted screen door. Vivian flicked the porch light switch on.

There was blood all over the snow, which had been swept over the deck by something large. They could see traces of black fur on the stairs, where the blood trail continued.

"There," Keith said. Something moved just out of reach of the light. They could see its basic shape. There were four limbs attached to a bulky body. Its head turned, its two eyes reflecting the glow of the porch. A loud roar burst from its lungs and it reared up.

Dillon shrieked and drew his pistol from his waistline, pointing it at the thing, and fired repeatedly. The loud bangs caused everyone to jump back. The thing cried out, yet advanced. He aimed for those glowing eyes and fired another few rounds. Blood spurted from the wounds. The thing let out a dying moan, then fell to its side, twitching in the snow as it died.

"Whew!" Dillon said, feeling shaken as well as triumphant. The rest of the group uncovered their ears.

"What the hell is it?" Keith asked. He remained on the deck next to Dillon, who kept his Glock pointed at the thing. Jeff stepped back into the cabin and came right back out with a flashlight in hand. He fired a beam of light on the thing.

"What I thought," he said. "It's a bear." It was four-hundred pounds at least. Its mouth was slack, the tongue curled in the snow. Its skull was carved open from the bullet wounds, seeping blood into the snow. Its feet continued to twitch, while its eyes stared off into nothingness. Jeff leaned closer with the flashlight. "What the hell is that?"

The bear's side had been severely gashed, exposing muscle tissue and even internal organs. The bear was already well on its way to dying when it found its way to their deck.

"What on earth did that?" Keith said.

"Well… I *did* shoot the bastard a dozen times…" Dillon said.

"No, you didn't do this," Jeff said. "It's almost as though something took a carving knife to this fella." He studied the wounds again. There were several, some traveling along its entire side. He could see the white of its rib bones through some of the slits. "Maybe it got into a fight with another bear." That didn't seem right, yet nothing else made sense. "Whatever happened, it got away and was probably looking for a place to hide." He shone his light into the yard, seeing the bear's bloody trail in the snow leading up to his deck. It had come from deep in the woods. He took a few steps further out, aiming the light into the trees. Dillon watched from the deck, while Vivian hurried down the stairs to join Jeff. The harsh chill of the air hardly affected her over the desire to see that Jeff was safe.

Jeff looked over his shoulder as she approached, keeping his light pointed out into the woods.

"What are you doing? Wait in the cabin where it's safe," he said.

"Only if you come back too," she whispered. A very subtle nudge of her elbow toward the deck expressed her concern. Jeff nodded.

"Okay," he whispered. Vivian's eyebrows raised. With a tremendous burst of energy, she raised her hands to her face and screamed, her eyes locked onto the beam of light. Jeff turned.

Something moved between the trees. He tried to follow it with the flashlight, but lost it in the canvas. He backed up alongside Vivian. Whatever it was, he only caught a glimpse. His mind tried to justify what he saw as possibly a spooked deer, though it didn't appear to be anything like it.

"Get back," he said, swaying his light back and forth. He saw empty branches, then the swaying sides of firs. Keith and Dillon leaned on the deck rail, their eyes glued to the scenery as Jeff redirected his light to the ground. There were tracks in the snow. Even from where he stood, he knew they weren't anything like hoofprints from a deer. He followed the short path with his light, until they stopped near a tree. There were no other prints around it. It was a dead end, as though the thing had simply disappeared.

Or…

Dillon was the first to gaze further up into the tree. Jeff aimed the light up. The branches leaned down, accommodating the weight of something large. The thick pine needles provided too much obstruction, keeping them from getting a good look. All they could see were long jagged claws prodding through the branches.

Dillon didn't wait. He pointed his Glock and fired madly.

An ear-piercing shriek tore through the air. The thing let go, splashing snow into a huge sparkling mist as it retreated behind the grouping of trees. Dillon kept squeezing the trigger, only to realize he had emptied his magazine. The slide was locked back, the air around the muzzle steaming hot. He looked back to the forest. The thing was gone. At least, it was out of their line of sight.

"Probably another bear," he mumbled.

"Maybe," Keith said. He was still breathing rapidly.

"Maybe," Dillon repeated. "Had to have been. What else could it be?" He let out a soft chuckle, which dissipated when he looked down at Vivian and Jeff. During the shooting, she had leapt into his arms. He stared as she hugged him, seeking Jeff for comfort rather than him. His wrist instinctively turned, aiming the Glock's muzzle down at Jeff. If that mag wasn't empty, he would have let off a shot and chalked it up as an accident during the shooting of the bear. But it was empty, and the extra magazines were packed somewhere with his belongings. The pleasure would have to wait.

"Let's get inside," Jeff said. He and Vivian walked back to the cabin and embraced the warmth of the fire.

"Vivian," Dillon barked, slamming the door shut behind him. "I need a drink."

Jeff leaned up to argue but was stopped by her hand on his shoulder.

"Fine," she said. "What kind of a drink?"

"Anything with alcohol. There's bourbon. Get that!"

"Okay," she said. She entered the kitchen, leaving Dillon and Jeff in another quiet standoff. A menacing smile creased the gang leader's face.

See? I'll always have control over her.

Vivian returned with a large glass full of booze for him. Dillon's smile shrank as she handed another glass to Jeff. He was about to protest until he saw her lift a third glass to her own lips.

"Bottom's up," she said. She started to drink. Jeff and Dillon glanced back at each other, then back at her. Jeff's eye went back to the kitchen. There, he noticed one of the cabinets was open a crack. It was the one with the medicine. He quickly started downing his alcohol. Sensing the manly challenge, Dillon followed, gulping large loads of the bourbon. In less than a few seconds, his glass was dry. He slammed it down on the table.

"Ha! Fucking amateur you are," he said victoriously. Jeff lowered his glass, which was halfway full.

"I suppose you win," he said. "I'm sure you're a man who can hold his drink." The crumpled up sleeping pills were already showing their initial signs of effect. That, or it may have just been the booze. Either way, Dillon was teetering slightly, well on his way into a deep slumber.

"I'll outdrink you any day of the week," Dillon said.

"Go for it," Jeff replied.

"Vivian!" Dillon said. "You know what to do!" She smiled and refilled his glass. He grinned again at Jeff, victorious in his own mind as he downed the glass.

CHAPTER 13

To their surprise, it took Dillon nearly a half-hour to finally succumb to his slumber. From his point of view, he was dozing off due to the booze. To him, such a thing was considered shameful. At the bars, he could outdrink anyone who raised a glass to him. Of course, that led to some of the fights that scarred his face. Regardless, he never backed down from a challenge, especially not from Jeff of all people.

He passed out on one of the sofas, his mouth hanging wide open. Before long, he was snoring.

Jeff and Vivian carefully moved him onto the bed. Jeff saw the duffle bags he had with him. He knelt down and unzipped one, spilling several pairs of clothes. "Damn," he said.

"What are you doing?" Vivian asked.

"Looking for any other guns," Dillon said. He stuffed the clothes back in and gave up. "He'll know we've been through his stuff. If he knows, he won't trust anything we do. Besides, I'll be hard pressed to find anything in these bags."

"Keith and Matt have guns anyway. He'd just take theirs," Vivian whispered. "Let's just wait. You think we can leave tomorrow night?"

"Maybe," Jeff said. "If that damn tree wasn't there, I'd chance it right now. I gotta chop it up and move it first. Until then, nobody's going anywhere."

They stepped out of Dillon's room and shut the door. Jeff took a seat on the couch and watched the window. His mind replayed the recent events that had just taken place outside.

"Something weird is going on," he said.

"What was that thing? A bear?" Vivian asked.

"I don't know what that thing was, but I've seen plenty of bears in my time. That was no bear. I saw those claws. They were like snakes. I've never seen anything like it. Besides, bears don't make a sound like that."

"I only caught a glimpse of it moving between the trees. Could it have been something else?" Vivian asked.

"I don't know what else it could've been," Jeff said. He was watching the window with unblinking eyes, seeing nothing but snow behind his own reflection.

"God, I just want to get out of here," Vivian said, shivering in her blanket. She sat beside him and leaned against his shoulder. "I feel like this place is haunted."

"If you ask any of the townspeople, that's probably what they'd tell you," Jeff said.

"What's the deal with this lake? It seems like it's forbidden to come here."

"I don't know the whole scoop," Jeff said. "Something happened back in '92. I guess this area was previously used as a campsite. A bunch of people came up here one winter. All of them turned up missing without a trace. Then, over the next couple of years, some weird stuff started happening in town. People were reported missing. A bunch of Ellisville residents left, some of them claiming the disappearances had something to do with a meteorite that reportedly crashed here. I don't know. It all sounds like nonsense to me. I've been up here plenty of times and I've never seen anything."

"A meteorite crashed here?"

"So they say. Some idiots think that it had an alien in it. Sounds to me like they'd been watching too much '50's sci-fi." *Yet, I saw something*. He wondered if his mind played tricks on him. It made sense, as it occurred after a sudden appearance by a black bear, an event which itself was preceded by a tense altercation with a violent murderous criminal. Maybe his mind was playing tricks on him.

"What if it only comes out in the winter?" Vivian asked. "I mean, think about it. Things move slower in the winter. The bears typically hibernate. Deer are usually hiding out. Maybe this thing has adapted to hunt in the cold when its prey is less adept at defending itself." Jeff nodded. Vivian continued, "You said you only come out in the summer. That's probably why you've never seen it."

"That's a hell of a thought," he said. He wanted to chuckle, but was afraid it'd come off as insulting. "Not sure I know of any animal that specifically comes out in winter."

"Well...were there any sightings reported during those disappearances?"

"Not that I know of," Jeff said.

"How many people disappeared?"

"Not sure. A dozen or so," Jeff said. Vivian guided his arm around her shoulders.

"You think you can get that tree cleared tomorrow?" she asked. Jeff could feel the tension that had her muscles knotted.

"I'll get on it first thing in the morning," he said. "First, I gotta move that dead bear."

"I just can't wait to get out of here," Vivian said.

"It'll happen," Jeff said. "But first, you need to get some sleep. We're thinking about this with boozed up minds. It was probably two bears that got in a fight with one another. The weather probably distorted our view of the other one. Nothing to worry about."

He and Vivian shared another kiss. Yet, her expression was still somber.

"Dillon had me set up to sleep in his room," she said. "I'll probably set up camp on this couch."

"Oh, no," Jeff said, standing her to her feet. "You'll take my room. *I'll* sleep out here."

"You sure?" Vivian asked.

"I'm sure. I gotta keep the fire going anyway," Jeff said. She embraced him with a warm hug, then made her way up the steps. She was halfway up when she looked back. She wanted to invite him up with her. It was a near-overwhelming drive. Yet, it was best they kept their newfound attraction as quiet as possible. And making love with people like Matt just a little ways down the hall was not appealing. After smiling once more, she completed her way up the steps.

Jeff waited until he heard the faint echo of the master bedroom door as it closed. He cracked the front door open again, wincing from the gust of icy air that invaded. He blasted his light around the yard, reassuring himself that nothing was there. Every movement from the trees played with his paranoid mind. That paranoia was fueled be a new realization...

He panned the light back down at the bear.

Shouldn't this fella be hibernating? Where's his den? After shining the light over the yard once more, he quietly approached the dead animal, keeping a hand on his revolver handle the whole time.

There was dirt in its fur. This bear had been hibernating...until something coaxed it out. Or forced it out.

His mind was going back into overdrive. Jeff made his way back up into the cabin and locked the door behind him. After throwing another log onto the fire, he went to the kitchen. Reaching high over the top of the shelf, he grasped the frame of his Remington 12-gauge shotgun. There was an oil kit nearby, which he also pulled down. Immediately, he went to work giving the gun a quick clean, which concluded with him loading it with shells and pumping the weapon to chamber one.

He sat in the chair, shotgun in lap, and glared at his reflection in the black window.

CREATURE OF LAKE SHADOW

CHAPTER 14

The worst of the storm had cleared the following morning, trailed by straggling clouds that dumped a light but steady flurry on Blessing County. Deputy Rick Beck drove his personal pickup truck, towing a trailer that carried his and Simon Mayer's snowmobiles. They had to use their personal ones, as Sheriff Glynn would never authorize they take the department's snowmobiles to the exterior of Circle Mountain, much less all the way to Lake Shadow. Rick noticed fresh tire tracks in the snow-covered road. Eddie Moore had likely beaten them out here.

"They didn't add enough creamer to this," Simon complained, sipping the Starbucks coffee Rick had promised him.

"If they don't fill the cup halfway with creamer, it's not enough for you," Rick said.

"I don't know why I agreed to this," Simon groaned, gazing out at the distant forest to his right.

"Hey, if I'm right, you could get a promotion out of this," Rick said. "Or at least a pay rise."

"I'll take the pay rise…and an extra week of vacation time," Simon said.

"Nothing's ever enough for you, is it?" Rick said.

"Speak for yourself, buddy," Simon replied. "You're the one who wants to play small-town detective and chase wild geese out in the land that time forgot over here."

"I'm telling you, I have a feeling…" Rick said.

"It's the same feeling that got you in trouble in Louisville," Simon reminded.

"Except I was right, and the wrong people were in power," Rick said, his voice bitter. He saw Eddie's truck up ahead. He was already beside it, mounting his snowmobile. He greeted them with a mock salute as Rick pulled the truck alongside his.

"Nice of you old ladies to join me," he said.

"I envy old ladies," Simon muttered. "If I were one, I'd be sitting on a couch at home, wrapped in a blanket. Wouldn't have to do anything. Definitely wouldn't be out here."

"You bring dignity to police everywhere," Rick joked as he handed Eddie his promised coffee.

"I'm honored," Simon replied. They worked together to get the snowmobiles out from the trailer. They started the engines and allowed them to warm up for a minute.

"Okay, Detective. How are we doing this?" Eddie asked.

"First thing's first. We'll follow the road up to the trees and take it along the path until we near the cabins."

"Won't they hear our engines?" Eddie asked.

"If anyone's even there," Simon added.

"Probably. Once we're close enough, we'll try and go on foot," Rick said.

"Oh, lovely," Simon griped. "You expect us to run out and apprehend the suspects. Make them make snow angels in the snow after handcuffing them?"

"What he means is what do we do IF we find the suspects hiding out there?" Eddie clarified. Rick could sense the doubt in his voice as well.

"Listen, if we find them, we won't apprehend them ourselves," Rick said. "We will alert Warren, who'll alert the state."

"Hopefully we see that chick with the tattoo," Simon said. "Because she'll be the only lead we'll have. Can't bring a whole army just because we see a group of people hiding out in a cabin. That's not evidence."

"No...you're right," Rick said. "But it might be peculiar enough to get a search warrant."

"What about the radio situation?" Eddie asked. "There's no way we'll be making calls on our phones out there. And our police radios are shit to begin with, I doubt they will get a signal out through those trees."

"Already taken care of," Rick said. He reached back in the truck and pulled out a long-range walkie talkie. "This radio can go out for twenty-three miles. It's a type often used by park rangers in terrains such as this. I've already programmed it to be in our Department's frequency, so in case we need to call out, this should do the trick."

"Should?"

"Well...the signal might still be a little static-y," Rick said. "But it's the best option we have." He tossed it to Eddie, who clipped it to his belt.

"Dude…you're gonna owe me ten coffees for being stupid enough to do this," Simon said.

"Why can't I just buy you a jug of creamer?" Rick said. All three of them shared a laugh, then boarded their snowmobiles. Engines roared as they sped out toward the thick forests of Circle Mountain.

CHAPTER 15

Jeff woke up with a frightened jolt. The air was freezing cold, far colder than it had been. The fire was low, but not out. He had maintained it during the night and watched the window until finally, at some point, he had fallen into a dreamless sleep.

He exhaled, seeing his breath billow in front of him. It wasn't his imagination. The air was icy cold. He stood up and moved to the nearest light switch. Nothing happened when he flicked it on.

"You've got to be kidding me," he said. He heard footsteps above him. At the mouth of the stairway was Matt, his eyes glassy and hair frizzy.

"What's going on? Why'd you turn the heat completely off?"

"I didn't," Jeff said. He moved to the kitchen and checked some other appliances. Nothing worked.

Keith was the next one to come down the steps. He was wearing two sweaters under his overcoat.

"Did the tank run out of propane?" he asked.

"It wasn't *that* low," Jeff said. They heard Dillon stirring in his bedroom. After a few seconds, he stumbled out into the living room, his clothes looking like they'd been in a blender. Jeff kept a watchful eye on him, noticing the bulge in the waistline of his sweater where he kept his pistol tucked. More than likely, he had reloaded it.

"What's going on now?" Dillon said, hungover.

"I'm figuring that out," Jeff said.

"Well, while you're figuring it out, I'm gonna take a piss!" Dillon strolled for the bathroom.

"Do it outside," Jeff said. Dillon laughed.

"You want me to piss icicles? It's five degrees out."

"There's no power, meaning it won't flush," Jeff said.

"What do you mean there's no power?!"

Jeff hung his head, frustrated.

"What it sounds like. As I stated before; I'm figuring it out. In the meantime, you'll have to do your business out there. I'm not gonna have the toilet backed up."

"Well, you better get on it, Mountain Man!" Dillon slammed the door shut behind him, his shoes crunching the broken glass from the screen door.

He made sure to go back to his shotgun before Dillon had a mind to go for it.

"What's with that?" Keith asked.

"I wasn't comfortable sleeping while bears and…other things… are running around outside my door," Jeff said.

"Things…" Matt's voice trailed off. Keith stepped in front of him.

"Matt…talk to me," he said, his voice calm. "You were out in the woods yesterday. Did you see anything?"

Matt stuttered. Memories of that cave flashed in his mind. He still questioned whether it was real or a figment of his drunken imagination. He thought about saying something. However, he was certain nobody would believe him. Hell, he wasn't even sure what he had seen. That cave could've belonged to that bear for all he knew. And that thing in the woods…it could've been a tree. The wind, snow, and general lack of sunlight had obscured his vision, making it easy for the imagination to take over.

"I tripped and got turned around, was all," he said.

"Matt, if there's something out there, I want to know," Keith said. Matt chuckled nervously. The shakes started their hideous return. Having slept for several hours, his body had been depraved of its incessant intake of alcohol. He turned for the steps.

"I'll be back."

"You saw nothing? You sure?"

"Yes! I'm sure!" Matt shouted. "I'm just a boozy drunkard! Now, as I said, I'll be back. You already know what I'm gonna do."

"Hang on," Jeff said. "I might need your help."

"Help?" Matt croaked. Jeff nodded, not even concerned with the shakes that were taking over the crook's body. "I'll…I said I'll be back! Just give me a minute." He darted up the steps, passing Vivian at the corner. At the same time, Dillon stepped back inside. He shot her a hard look as she came down the stairs.

"What are you doing up there?" he snarled. Vivian's jaw dropped, unsure of how to answer.

"I let her use my bed," Jeff said. He went to the back of the kitchen and opened the fuse panel. Nothing seemed to work.

"Oh, I see," Dillon growled. "Had yourselves a little 'shenanigan' did ya?!"

"Dillon, relax. I slept down here on the chair," Jeff said. Dillon kept his eyes locked on his woman. Dillon eased up. He'd deal with Vivian later.

"I'll give you credit for working late, Mountain Man," he said. "I see you've already moved the bear." Jeff looked back at him.

"I didn't move the bear," he said.

"You didn't? Then where is it?"

Jeff pulled on his boots and coat and darted out the door. The snowfall had decreased into a mild flurry, though the wind was still coursing like an angry beast. He leaned over the porch rail and looked. There was no bear, only an indentation in the snow where it had lain.

"What are those?" Vivian asked. She pointed at a series of tracks that led back into the woods. It was the same direction as the 'thing' that they saw running in the woods. The footprints were unlike anything Jeff had ever seen. The main body of each one was somewhat similar to a person's, though larger. However, each one had curved extensions at the front, like the horns of a bull. Alongside those tracks was a small trench in the snow, leading from where the bear had been.

"Okay, this is getting bizarre," Keith said.

"Yes it is," Vivian said.

"Let's get the hell out of here," Dillon added.

"How?" Keith said. "We're blocked in, remember?" He pointed a finger to the road. Dillon growled, as if the tree had fallen deliberately.

"Fuck this place. Fuck these woods. And fuck you, Mr. Mountain Man, for bringing us to this fucking place, in these fucking woods!"

Jeff ignored the tirade and hurried down the steps, holding his shotgun at his shoulder. He turned the corner and saw several tracks around the back of his cabin. The propane tank appeared to be untouched, though the tracks indicated that something had walked around it recently.

He continued around the back, followed closely by Keith. He had his own pistol gripped tightly with both hands. They stepped around to the back of the cabin. There, they found the generator in shambles. The side panel had been ripped free, exposing the internal components, which had been shredded to bits. The alternator had been torn free completely, along with the voltage regulator and engine. Long grooves lined the debris in irregular motions.

"I don't suppose that can be fixed," Dillon asked.

"No chance," Jeff said.

"What the hell did this?" Vivian said.

"Same thing that left these tracks," Jeff said. All around the busted generator were several of those strange tracks.

"Let's move that tree and let's get out of here," Keith said.

"And go where?" Dillon said. "It's probably another bear."

"Bears don't eat each other, genius!"

"Maybe it wasn't completely dead," Dillon said.

"Alright, everyone calm down. We can't go anywhere at the moment. I still gotta take that tree apart, and that'll take a few hours at least," Jeff said.

"It's not like I have a forklift or a bulldozer to push it aside. We'll have to cut through the branches first. Then cut away sections of the trunk. We'll have to haul each piece out of the way... we have a lot to do before we can even think about leaving."

"Will we be safe inside?" Vivian asked.

"Yes," Jeff said. He wasn't sure, but there was no point in getting her even more worried. "I'll have to go get more firewood first. What we cut last night is almost out. With this wind, it won't be long before that cabin is practically an ice cube."

"Why can't we use the wood from the fallen tree?"

"It's unseasoned wood," Jeff said. "It won't burn properly. We're better off using the wood from the stack."

"Dillon and I will go get the wood," Keith said.

"Ha!" Dillon said.

"Dillon, come on man! This is no time to be..."

"I'm paying *you*," Dillon said. "Not the other way around. I'm not staying out in this freezing cold any longer than I have to." He stomped his way back to the front entrance then stuck his head inside. "MATT! Get your ass down here!"

"Dillon, I'm not sure it's a good idea," Keith said, trying to keep his voice level. "I think Matt's not feeling too well. Maybe it's the cold, or he's traumatized from what happened at the bank. But I think something happened while he was out last night..."

"His problem is that he spends too much time sucking on a bottle!" Dillon snapped. "I wouldn't trust him if he told us it was snowy out! No, it's time he did something useful." He stepped further in. "MATT! I'm not going to call you down again!"

Finally, like a timid little mouse, Matt peeked around the top of the stairway.

"Get your coat. You're going to gather wood with Keith."

"What? But I..."

Dillon's face wrinkled. "You arguing with me?"

Matt stammered. "Uh...no, no...just let me get my boots." He ducked back to his room.

Keith was shaking his head. "Jesus, Dillon, why can't you do it? You're bigger and stronger. It'll be done faster."

"Nah, I have other matters to attend to," Dillon said.

"What matters?"

"Not your concern," Dillon said. That was all Keith needed to hear. He sighed audibly, knowing Dillon was planning on having a meeting with Vivian while Jeff was cutting the tree. He had been near those confrontations before and they were never pleasant. Those memories brought shame, as he was always too intimidated to step in and stop it. Whenever he'd ask Dillon, he'd get the same response he just heard.

Matt wobbled as he stumbled down the steps.

"I'm coming. I'm coming," he said, his voice slurred. Keith leaned in toward Dillon.

"Maybe I should just do it alone. He shouldn't be handling sharp axes in this condition."

"He's going," Dillon hissed. Keith wrinkled his nose. The jerk was looking for privacy, which confirmed another fear he had for Vivian. If Dillon was angry at her, part of her 'reconditioning' would be to perform a sexual favor. And yet again, Keith was too much of a coward to intervene, and he hated himself for it.

He walked past Dillon and grabbed his coat from the closet.

"Come on, Matt," he said. "Let's make this quick." He realized the irony in his statement. With Matt, such a physical job like wood cutting would not be quick. Probably something Dillon was counting on.

They walked to the shed. Jeff was already inside, filling the chainsaw up with fuel.

"Just follow our tracks from last night," Jeff said. "They'll lead you right to the place."

"Thanks," Keith said. "How far is it?"

"Maybe a quarter-mile."

"Hey, um," Keith revealed his Glock, "will a nine-millimeter kill a bear?"

"Short answer is yes," Jeff said. *Though those aren't bear tracks,* his mind continued. "Just be careful with your aim. It'll take more than one bullet." Keith nodded. "You want me to go with you?"

"No," Keith said. He glanced worriedly at the cabin. "It's best you get started on the tree. Or else Dillon will flip. Besides, you're the one best suited to keep an eye on things here." Jeff gave a slight nod, understanding what he meant. He wondered why Keith, a man with half-decent judgement, ended up in a group like this.

Keith and Matt grabbed the axes and tote then started for the lake. Jeff lifted the chainsaw and walked across the front of the cabin. Vivian was on the porch, worriedly watching him. And behind her, somewhere in that cabin, was Dillon, planning God-knows-what.

CHAPTER 16

"Hey Eddie! Hold up!"

Eddie could hardly hear Rick's calls through the two-way radio, causing him to drive several yards ahead. When he finally did hear Rick's instruction for him to stop, he turned back and parked his snowmobile along the edge of the road. Not that there was any road left. Right now, there was simply a fifteen-foot gap between the trees that had been completely blanketed in snow and ice.

Rick and Simon were standing near the tree line, staring at a portion of snow that appeared to have been mashed up. There were signs of tire tracks, as well as general shallowness compared to the surrounding snow, as though it had been dug out.

"Looks like somebody had a little spin-out," Rick said.

"And they had snow shovels on hand," Simon said.

"Holy shit," Eddie said, impressed. "That means somebody actually came out here."

"With intent to stay a while," Rick added.

"We still don't know for sure if it's the perps, so we can't call the Sheriff yet," Simon said. There was a change of tone in his voice. Despite expressing doubt, he was now starting to believe the possibility that Rick's hunch might have been a good one.

"Then let's get on it," Rick said. "Just a reminder: these bastards are armed and dangerous. They've already killed two people, one of them a cop. Which means they probably won't hesitate to put a round in us."

"I'm well aware," Eddie said. He got back on his snowmobile and completed a U-turn, driving further ahead without waiting for his buddies. Rick and Simon quickened their pace in an effort to catch up.

They traveled the winding path, enduring the icy blast of wind that assaulted every square inch of their bodies. Rick and Simon traveled side-by-side, keeping a close eye on the road for any clues. The snow and wind had eliminated almost every trace of tire tracks during the night. Additionally, they had to avoid debris on the road. The storm had shaken an array of branches from the trees and scattered them over the surface.

"Fuck!" Simon muttered, feeling the reverberation of his snowmobile hitting a branch.

"Careful," Rick said. They weaved around a few obstacles, then caught up with Eddie, who had stopped at a fork in the road. It was clear from how he was staring at it that he wasn't sure which way to go.

"I wanna say they went right," he said. "The snow on the left looks smoother to me. Less disturbed. However you want to describe it."

"I get what you mean," Rick said. "However, how do we describe this?" he worked his way several meters down the small hill and brushed the snow from the side of a tree, fully revealing the scraping in the bark. There were traces of white paint embedded in the marking, almost grey in color. The vehicle was not very old.

"I don't believe old Steve gave a description of the vehicle they were driving, did he?"

"No. He did not," Eddie answered.

"Somebody clearly went this way," Rick said. He knelt down and dug through the snow around the foot of the tree. "Ah ha!" He stood straight, holding a broken piece of bumper as though holding a trophy. "Had a little run-in with a tree, it looks like."

"Should we call Sheriff Glynn now?" Simon asked. "You did say simply finding evidence that someone was in these cabins during this storm, along with Steve's testimony, might be enough to get a search warrant."

"I'm aware," Rick said. "But this piece of bumper could belong to anybody. Let's continue down this way, see if we can spot any trace of a group of people, one of them being a female. If it turns out it's not them, we'll check the other cabin."

"Fine," Simon said. As Rick approached his snowmobile, Eddie was already roaring his engine.

"Meet you there," he said.

"Don't get too close," Rick called after him, his words landing on deaf ears. *Fool. Good work ethic, but a little too eager. Then again...who am I to judge? I'm the one who brought them out here.*

He got back on his snowmobile and followed the deputy, traveling alongside Simon. They worked their way to the bottom of the hill then started the series of bends. Simon completed a turn, only to curse when he saw the jagged edge of a large branch protruding from the tree line. Eddie had avoided it, but Simon was a little too close.

"Shit-shit-shit-shit!" He hit the branch. The snowmobile jolted upward. The engine crackled and popped. It was immediately clear that something was loose. He slowed to a stop. Rick parked right behind him.

"You all right?" he asked.

"I will be when you buy me a new snowmobile!" Simon grunted. They looked to Eddie, who continued to speed off toward the cabin.

"Hey!" Rick grabbed the radio. "Eddie, hold up!" There was no response. "Damn knucklehead." He helped Simon open the engine, and they were immediately met with a ball of hot air which clouded their vison.

Eddie slowed as he saw a larger spacing between the trees. He could see the lake from where he stood. The cabin had to have been near. He carefully steered his snowmobile to the left, hiding it behind the wall of trees. It was then that he finally realized that Simon and Rick were not right behind him.

He grabbed his radio. "Hey, guys?" There was no response. The internal debate started in his mind. Wait here or go back and find them? A third option crossed his mind: start the investigation.

"They'll see my trail," he whispered to himself. "They'll know I'm here." He crouched low and crossed the road into the opposite maze of trees. Like a spy in a foreign land, he worked his way to the cabin, careful not to get his coat snagged on the hundreds of branches and twigs in his way.

After three hundred feet, he could see the two-story cabin. He watched quietly, desperately looking for any movement.

"Come on," he whispered, begging for any of the crooks to step outside. He was desperate to be the one to find them. He would play it up in his resume, and finally get the hell out of this department into bigger and better things.

There was no movement. What he did see was out of place. There was an enormous truck in front of the cabin. At first, he assumed it was a large van, which seemed suitable. A gang of criminals would need a larger vehicle for transport. But then he noticed the rounded shape near the back. It was a small propane tanker. Immediately after came the realization that it was right in the middle of the front yard, nowhere near the propane tank.

Eddie moved in for a closer look. The truck was smashed against a tree. His heart began to punch his insides. Something was not right. He looked over his shoulder. Rick and Simon were nowhere to be seen. He tried his radio again.

"Guys?" There was no answer. Damn trees. Damn twelve-year old radios. He glanced back, examining the pickup truck that was parked near the cabin. In all likeliness, it wasn't the escape vehicle for a bunch of bank robbers. Which, to him, made the situation seem stranger. Something clearly happened here.

He had his Glock unholstered now. Eddie sucked in a deep breath as he approached the crime scene.

"Shit!" Simon exclaimed, withdrawing his hand from a sharp piece of metal. The hull had been breached. They couldn't quite detect what had been damaged specifically, especially with the hot air from the engine filling their vision with mist. "Just my luck. I didn't even want to come out here."

"Let's just hold off for now," Rick said. "Get on mine. Let's catch up with Eddie, and we'll worry about this on our way back."

"Yeah?" Simon snarled. "How do you expect us to take this back? Drag it?"

"I..." Rick was feeling awkward and overwhelmed. "I will take care of it, I promise. But first, let's make sure Eddie doesn't get himself shot. The kid's a little too eager to make a name for himself."

"Fine," Simon said. He took the seat behind Rick. "Bear in mind, this is the only time we'll *ever* find ourselves in this position."

"You think *I* like it?" Rick retorted. He drove them around the bend, carefully dodging debris as he caught up with Eddie.

Eddie was at the propane tank. A gust of wind made him jump. He felt like he was walking on haunted grounds. He gulped as he saw traces of torn clothing sticking out from the snow. There was blood crusted around them, forming dark red icicles.

In his mind, the reputation of Circle Mountain had been earned. Already, he vowed to never return. His eyes turned toward the propane truck. Fear gripped his heart. The driver's side door had been ripped free completely. Frozen blood had formed thick streams over the seat and steering wheel.

"Screw this," he said. He started to back away. At that point, he heard the rumble of an engine. He turned toward the road and ran, not noticing the strange tracks near the trees.

He approached the tree line and waited. The engine stopped, yet they were still out of sight at the other side of the bend. *Damn it, they stopped where I got off.*

There was a new rumbling sound. His hopeful mind thought it was them again. Maybe they decided to say 'screw-it' and drive the rest of the way down to save time.

But this sound was different. It wasn't like an engine, instead it sounded more...organic. Iced-up snow crunched loudly behind him. The sun's glare turned to mild darkness around him. Eddie's muscles cramped. The shadow was an impossible shape, almost human-like, but not.

In a lightning motion, he spun on his heel and extended his weapon. The thing was faster. Long, dagger-like fingers punched through his body with the ease of a blowtorch through butter. His scream came out as nothing more than a gag as his lungs were ruptured. It lifted his spasming body off the ground. His gun cracked the air, the bullets flying aimlessly as his arm flailed.

"What the hell was that?" Simon said. It had only been moments since he and Rick found Eddie's vacant snowmobile. They felt for their guns as a series of loud cracks rippled through the air.

"He's in trouble!" Rick said. "Come on!" Both officers drew their weapons and raced along the curve of the road as fast as they could.

Eddie twitched, the gun falling from his hand. Blood pooled beneath his feet, melting the snow it landed on. As the life left his body, Eddie glared into the horrid, insectoid face of his killer. Multiple eyes stared back at him. It hissed, then twisted its claws, tearing his insides up further. Determined to feed, it turned and darted for the lake, intent on bringing its catch to its lair.

The two deputies cleared the bend, pointing their weapons into the lawn. Rick took the right while Simon stood left. Being inexperienced in firefights, or dangerous situations in general, he strayed behind while his partner entered the scene.

They immediately saw the huge pool of blood in the snow, and the trail leading out to the lake. Alongside them were several strange footprints, almost like a human's...yet not.

"Oh my God," Rick said. Eddie's gun was in the snow. The realization of what just occurred was sinking in. "Oh Jesus. Holy Christ...EDDIE!" He grabbed his radio. "Eddie, where are you? Eddie, answer me, goddamnit!" He lowered his radio and yelled again. "EDDIE!"

Simon gradually approached, looking like he was about to be sick.

"Dude, let's call back-up," he said.

"Eddie had the damn radio," Rick said. He saw Simon getting frantic, then grabbed him by the shoulders. "Get it together, man!" He gave him a hard shake. "Focus. You're in this situation now!" Simon nodded. They moved around the front of the house. The first course of action was to secure the area.

Simon stepped through the busted doorway, panned his weapon across, then grew pale as he saw the owner's severed head laying on the floor.

"Oh…ohhh," he stumbled back, bumping into Rick.

"Oh, GOD!"

"Something's not right, man. This is some really fucked up shit." Simon continued backing away, right to the crashed propane truck. He turned around. Suddenly, his body went numb.

Rick did a brief check of the rest of the house then hurried out onto the porch. There, he watched his partner staring hypnotically at the ravaged corpse inside the truck. He approached and pulled his partner away. But it was too late; the image was burnt into his brain.

The skull was completely exposed, with no eyes or other features other than some frozen pink stuff inside. The clothes had been ripped from the torso, revealing broken bones protruding from a meatless corpse.

Simon dry-heaved, something Rick was close to doing himself. Despite being accustomed to seeing dead bodies in various stages of decomposition, this was something else entirely.

"We have to go after Eddie," he said.

"Huh?" Simon looked back at him. "I'm not going anywhere but back."

"Eddie might still be alive. Whoever did this, carried him off."

"You think a person did this?" Simon squawked, pointing at the skeletal corpse.

"I've seen acid burns before," Rick said. "It's odd, but it makes sense that that's what they used." His eyes went to the rib and chest area. "Though, these don't look like acid burns here…BUT it doesn't matter. We gotta go after him."

Simon stood back up. His nauseous expression turning into anger.

"This is YOUR fault!" He shoved Rick back.

"Re—" Rick clamped his mouth shut. Telling an angry person to relax only worked to stir the fire. "Maybe it is. But the fact is, we can't leave Eddie out here. It'll take a while for help to arrive." Simon seethed for another moment, then finally cooled off. Rick was right. Simon kept a firm grip on his weapon as he followed the tracks down to the lake.

They appeared to take a right turn once they neared the shore. Every few feet were a few droplets of Eddie's blood.

"Could this be something else?" he asked. "Like a bear?"

"I don't know. I don't think so," Rick said. "It doesn't seem right. There are only black bears around here, and they don't generally go after people."

"You think it was those people?" Simon asked.

"All I know is that they've killed two people already," Rick replied.

"But these footprints…" Simon's voice trailed off. Rick understood what he wanted to say. The tracks were big and oddly shaped. Yet, they maintained the basic stride of a human. The reports did indicate that one of the robbers was a fairly large individual. The oddity in the toes could easily be from something sticking out from the boots.

He calmed his nerves and guided his partner along the shore. Whoever did this was going to pay dearly.

CHAPTER 17

Jeff was in the midst of starting his chainsaw when the faint echoes entered his eardrums. He had been around firearms long enough to recognize the sound, even from a couple of miles off.

Vivian stepped down from the porch.

"Was that what I think it was?" she asked. Jeff nodded. Vivian hugged her chest and looked around. "Where'd it come from?"

"I think from Schroeder's cabin," Jeff said.

"What could he be shooting at? What's going on?"

Jeff placed the chainsaw down in order to comfort her.

"Hey, it'll be fine. I promise," he said. She threw herself on him and hugged him tight.

"There's something going on," she said.

"I know," he answered. "Just bear with me. I'll get you out of this. But I need you to wait and let me do my work. If we are to leave, I've gotta cut away this tree."

Vivian nodded and slowly backed away. Jeff gave one more look over the horizon. There was no way to see Schroeder's cabin from where he stood. He never met the guy, only knew him by name, but otherwise didn't know anything about him. Yet, he doubted those gunshots were from recreational shooting. The wind blew, sending a barrage of icy particles into his face, reaffirming that thought.

He started the chainsaw and pressed the blade to the tree.

Keith stared across the lake after hearing the strange echoes. He held the axe at shoulder-level, originally poised to strike the cylinder-shaped log in front of him. Now, it was a defensive posture.

"You think those were gunshots?" he said. Matt didn't respond. The idiot didn't care. He was lost in a drunken abyss, chugging away at his flask. He had paused when he heard the sounds, but in the several minutes of silence that followed, he continued in his normal ways. Keith felt himself getting irritated, but knew yelling at him would do nothing. "Grab the tote. I'll slice the pieces and you fill them up. It'll go faster this way."

Matt wobbled back and forth. He glanced into the woods, then back behind him toward the rock wall. He couldn't see much of it due to the trees. Only its ragged incline which neared the lake.

Keith split the wood then looked back at him.

"Come on, man!" he shouted. He followed Matt's gaze. "What are you looking at?"

"Nothing," Matt said. He picked up the tote bag and tossed in a few chunks of firewood. Keeping a watchful eye on him, Keith split another piece. The branches swayed above him as another hard breeze cut through. Snow, acorns, and twigs rained down with a barrage of snow, sending icy snowflakes into his eyes. Keith stepped back and wiped his face with his sleeve. "Damn, freaking weather." The wind continued, causing the branches above to clatter. A few larger pieces rained down near the log pile. The branches were iced over and weighed down, making them prone to snapping.

Keith stood by, deciding to hold off until the breeze stopped. Better to wait a few moments and not risk getting clunked on the head.

Vivian was on the porch steps, shivering from the weather's continuous onslaught. She begged for the clouds to break up and provide them some decent sunshine. At least then the surrounding forest wouldn't seem quite so haunting.

The door creaked. Broken glass crunched under Dillon's boots as he stepped outside. Vivian cringed at the sound of his voice.

"Vivian, I need to talk to you for a moment." His voice was barely audible over the chainsaw's grind.

"Can it wait?" she asked.

"What?" Dillon put a hand to his ear.

"Can it—"

"I can't hear you," he interrupted. He came down the steps, hand still to his ear. His eyes briefly went to Jeff, whose back was turned. The saw was midway through the tree trunk and passing through quickly. He had only a few moments.

Dillon's hands lashed out, grabbing Vivian by her shoulders. He spun her around until her back was to him, then quickly dulled her scream by cupping her mouth.

"Your behavior lately has been very ill-advised," he growled in her ear. He lifted her off the ground and carried her up the porch. Vivian kicked her legs and twisted her body, but could not outmatch Dillon's superior strength. He dragged her inside, slamming the door shut behind them.

Swinging her like a ragdoll, Dillon slammed her hard into the nearest wall. Her whole body jolted from the intense impact. Vivian's struggle stopped. Her head throbbed, having bounced off the wooden wall. Dillon's fingers closed over her throat.

"Stop," she said.

"You've been fucking around with Mountain Man, haven't you?" he said.

"No...I—" Vivian gagged as his grip tightened.

"You think I'm gonna pass out after two bourbons?" he said. "Is it any coincidence that you come down from *his* bedroom the morning after you spiked my drink?" Vivian tried to answer, but he wouldn't let her. Finally, Dillon threw her onto the bed.

Vivian coughed with her hand at her throat. It wouldn't be long before another bruise would form where his fingers had been. She looked back at him. He placed his gun on the night table, then reached to undo the button of his jeans.

"Fuck yourself," she said. His eyebrows raised. This newfound defiance only elevated his suspicions.

"Take off your pants," he demanded. Vivian did nothing except scoot back. Her eyes glanced over to the Glock, something that Dillon noticed. He lashed out and grabbed her by the wrists.

"Okay, you bitch. I've had enough of you. First, I'm gonna give you what you deserve. Then, I'll take care of your new boyfriend. Then, you two can remain together in this cabin. I'll even arrange for your corpses to snuggle on the couch!"

"Here's an arrangement for ya."

In his rage, Dillon never heard the door open. He glanced behind him just in time to see the white knuckles of Jeff's closed fist before it plowed into his nose. Dillon staggered back then threw his hands up. Another blow caught him in the chin, and another at his waistline. Dillon threw a blind swing. Jeff leaned back, letting it miss, then closed with another hard punch to the jaw. This one knocked Dillon onto his back.

"Get out of here, Viv," Jeff said. She grabbed the Glock and ran out of the room. Dillon sprang to his feet, ready to charge, only to find the muzzle of a loaded revolver pointed right at his nose. Behind it was an icy glare, as cold as the wind outside. "Please do it. I dare ya," he warned.

"Can we hurry this up, please," Matt groaned. The breeze finally concluded, allowing Keith to step back to the log pile to continue cutting.

"It'd move faster if you'd lay off that stuff for thirty seconds," Keith said.

"Hey man," Matt said.

"Don't 'hey man' me," Keith said. "Nobody's been more sympathetic than I have regarding your alcoholism. But it needs to stop, Matt. Something's going on around here, and you're worried about this shit!" He snatched the flask, which Matt immediately snatched back.

"To hell with you!" Matt said. "You don't think I'm good for anything? I'll split all these logs right now."

"Matt...careful!" Keith winced as Matt picked up the other axe, inadvertently waving it across his chest. The drunkard ignored him and shakily propped a new log on the stand. He raised his axe over his head, the sudden shift in weight making him teeter backwards. Keith stepped in and grasped his arms to keep him from slicing either of them open. "Relax! Relax!" He steadied the nervous fella. "Matt, you've always been strange. But you've been acting *particularly* strange since last night. What happened? Did Dillon's shooting of the cop fry your brain? Or did you see something last night? I'm not making fun, I need to know!"

"I don't...I don't know if I saw anything. The booze makes me see things like..." His gaze moved high into the tree. He froze. "Oh Lord."

"Matt what are you talking ab—" Keith felt another onslaught of snow falling down on him. Yet, there was no breeze at the moment. A moment later, the icy sensation was accompanied by something warm. Droplets hit his shoulders like rain. He looked down on himself. Little red rivers ran over his coat. "What the—"

Keith looked up.

It was twenty feet above him, its double-jointed legs propped on the arm of a branch. Its triangular insectoid face was staring back down on him with numerous marble-shaped eyes. It stood like a man, though there was nothing human about it. Its mouth was red with the blood of its latest catch. It was recognizable only by the clothing. It was eating a human.

The creature dropped its meal, which plummeted to the snow. Adrenaline soared through Keith's veins. He staggered back, completely lost in a world of terror. The creature descended, landing directly in front of him. Two arms lashed at him, its hands containing three jagged digits, each of them sixteen inches of razor sharp claw. All six of them found their way into Keith's abdomen.

Keith retched and spasmed as those claws pulled away from each other. Bones snapped, veins popped, and muscles and organs ripped as Keith was pulled into two pieces. Matt shrieked as blood splashed his face and body. Keith came apart as though cleaved down the middle with a broadsword. His head dangled lifelessly to the open side, while organs spilled and intestines uncoiled into the snow. Covered in his friend's blood, Matt fled, kicking up waves of snow as he went for the cabin.

The beast watched the second creature flee. It was going into that artificial structure which it had stalked during the night. Soon enough, it would track it down, along with the rest of its group. But first, it would take its new prize back to its lair. It staked the two halves onto one claw, then picked up the torso of its latest prize. The legs had already been stripped to the bone. The contents of the belt and jacket spilled into the snow. They were inedible. Useless. As were the strange materials that covered the flesh. The creature would strip the rest of them off soon, then gorge.

With large bounds, it moved across the lake.

"I'm telling you, I heard screams," Rick said. He and Simon quickened their pace, weaving between several fat trees along the shoreline. There was a clearing up ahead. Behind the trees was movement.

"I see something," Simon said.

"Me too," Rick said. They hurried to the right, keeping just out of sight as they studied the moving figure. Rick pulled his binoculars and took a look. He watched the man running with an axe in hand. He repeatedly glanced over his shoulder. "Holy God!" The man's face was smothered in fresh blood as though it had been sprayed on him with a garden hose. He handed the glasses to Simon. He watched, catching glimpses between the trees. The bloodied man ran in an unstable motion, tripping repeatedly while still holding the axe, which too was covered in blood.

"Holy fuck!" Simon said. "Dude, we've got a psycho murderer on our hands!"

"Let's move in," Rick said. "He came from that way. Let's see if we can find Eddie." *Or what's left of him.*

They moved to the left, keeping an eye out for any other people. They came across the stack of logs. Simon covered his mouth and turned away after seeing the huge pool of blood and intestines on the ground. Even Rick was lightheaded.

"Oh…my God."

Several feet away was Eddie's gun, along with shreds of his jacket and pants, a boot, radio, and the long-range radio. Rick snatched it from the snow and brushed it off. He adjusted the volume, extended its antennae, and began transmitting.

"Unit Five to Dispatch, come in. We have an officer down at Lake Shadow. We need assistance here on the double."

There was a brief pause. Clearly, the dispatcher and all units listening in were caught off guard by the unexpected news.

"This is Sheriff Glynn. What's going on?"

"Sheriff, we've got a mad killer up here on Circle Mountain. There's at least two civilians dead, and Deputy Moore has been KIA."

"Jesus. All units, converge on Ellisville. Dispatch, get the county to send their plows. Otherwise, it'll take us a hundred years to get out there. And call every off-duty officer. They're on duty now. If they complain, have them call me. Deputy Beck, are we aware of how many suspects there are?"

"We've only seen one for sure, but I suspect there's others, judging by the way we've seen things. It'd be hard for one person to pull all of this off."

"If you can, evaluate the situation more. But do not engage unless necessary. There's already one cop dead."

"Affirmative," Rick said. "We'll be out of contact. Don't want these guys hearing everyone's radio chatter."

"Fine. Just keep us informed."

"Ten-four." Rick switched the volume to its lowest setting. He glanced back at Simon. "You game for getting a closer look?"

Simon glanced at the guts, then at his pistol, which trembled in his hands. Never before did he think he'd ever have to draw his weapon, and here he was initiating a manhunt. It was time to be a real cop.

"Yep…" he said. "I'm good. Let's do it."

"Take it slow," Rick said. "Maintain three-sixty degrees of awareness." They gradually worked their way up the hill, watching each step not to step on anything that would snap or pop, or otherwise give away their position.

CHAPTER 18

"Alright, you dumb fuck, step on out," Jeff said. He had backed into the living room, his revolver fixed on Dillon's chest. The gang leader stared him straight in the eye. He hesitated, deciding on whether to test Jeff's resolve. Finally, he raised his hands slowly and followed him out into the living room. He played a hundred scenarios in his mind on how he could possibly disarm his new enemy and kill him.

He glanced at Vivian, then back at Jeff. A sneer creased his bloodied face.

"Keep in mind, Mountain Man; every time you set up camp…" he gestured at Vivian, "I was there first." His sneer transformed into a crude smile, then into a kissing motion at Vivian.

"Shut up," Jeff said. "If I was a less decent person, I'd shoot you in the face right here. Unfortunately, I have too much patience."

"You'll need it if you wanna hook up with that whore," Dillon said. "Hey, next time you go cave diving, you'll probably find traces of its former inhabitant."

"Good God, you're sick," Vivian said.

"You used to live for it, baby," he said.

"Yeah, somehow I doubt that," Jeff said. "We've talked enough. Turn around and put yourself against the wall."

"What? You a cop?"

"No, but that's where you'll be going." Jeff nudged the revolver to the wall between the bedroom and bathroom. "Do it." Dillon simply smiled, as if daring him to shoot. Jeff cocked the hammer back. "I won't say it again." That smile slowly faded. Dillon suspected he had underestimated his host. Clearly, he knew nothing of what Jeff had seen and done in his Army days.

The door burst open, causing all three to jump. Jeff saw Matt stagger in, axe in hand, with blood painted down his front. In that moment, his aim waivered off of Dillon, who instantly sprang. Arms wrapped around his waist as the muscular gang member threw him to the floor. The hairpin trigger squeezed back, sending a round into the ceiling.

Dillon hammered a fist into Jeff's jaw, then grabbed for the revolver. Jeff shifted his body weight and plowed an elbow under Dillon's ribs. The men rolled, both of them fighting for a grip on the weapon. A moment later, they were on their feet, with Dillon locking his arms around Jeff's neck. Unable to get a shot and realizing the crazed fiend was about to get the better of him, Jeff launched the revolver, past Matt's head, out through the open doorway. Locked in Dillon's grip, Jeff twisted his body and ducked low, slipping through the headlock. A fist found Dillon's jaw, which was then followed by a kick to the ribs. Dillon reeled back over the arm of the sofa. Flailing his arms frantically, he grabbed for anything he could. His fingers found the neck of an empty bourbon bottle. Jeff saw the swing coming and crossed his hands over his face. The bottle struck his forearms, not yet shattering. Dillon struck again with a wide swing, this time missing completely. An elbow to the face drove him back again.

Dillon flicked his tongue like a snake, wiggling some loosened teeth. He raised the bottle and advanced for another attack.

"Stop!" Vivian yelled, pointing her pistol at Dillon's face. He froze for a moment, breathing heavily, watching her. She had the weapon properly gripped, with one finger resting on the trigger. He took another deep breath then slowly turned to face her. That evil smile reappeared. He took a small step toward her. Vivian's hands shook. "I said stop. I WILL do it!"

"I bet you will," Dillon said. He moved in closer. Vivian squeezed her eyes shut and pressed the trigger. There was no gunshot. "Oops," Dillon said. "Looks like I forgot to chamber a round when I loaded it." He lunged and snatched the gun from her hand before throwing her to the floor. He pulled the slide back then aimed it down.

Before he could shoot, Jeff grabbed the tray table and hurled it through the air. It struck him on the forehead, sending him reeling backwards into the bathroom.

Jeff dashed for the door, grabbing Vivian along the way. Dillon leaned up and fired a few gunshots wildly, nicking Matt's shoulder.

"Come on!" They hurried onto the porch and jumped over the rail. Jeff found the revolver and picked it up, then moved around the corner where he left the shotgun.

"Where do we go?" Vivian asked.

"Into the trees. It'll be harder for them to keep track," Jeff said.

"Where's Keith?" Vivian said. "And why was Matt covered in blood?"

"I don't know, Viv,' he said. "Let's just worry about getting out of here."

Dillon stomped out of the bathroom, tearing the partially open door off the hinges to get it out of his way. He saw the blood-soaked Matt, clutching his injured shoulder.

"What the hell happened to you? Where the hell is Keith?!"

Matt stammered, completely dumbfounded by everything that occurred within the last ten minutes. Dillon grabbed him by the shirt.

"Where is he?!" he yelled.

"He—" Matt struggled to get any words out.

"What? You autistic or something? Fucking talk!" He gave Matt another hard shake.

"He's dead!" Matt squeaked.

"Dead?! What the fuck do you mean *dead*?!"

"Some—something...OUT THERE!!" Matt pointed into the trees. "There's something—it got him! It—I...I-I-I...I saw it! A monster! A devil!" His jaw shivered.

"What the hell are you talking about, you boozing drunkard?!" Dillon shouted, shaking Matt by the shoulders. The scrawny thief fell into complete hysterics, cupping his hands over his ears and yelling. The axe clanged against the floor. Dillon picked it up, eyed the blade, then looked outside. Jeff and Vivian had just ducked into the trees. He looked at the axe again.

Hmmm, this might be fun. Shoot him in the leg. Then make Vivian watch as I take this bad boy to him. Piece-by-piece.

Dillon started out the door, leaving Matt cowering by the furniture.

"It was a devil. We are paying for our sins."

"Whatever," Dillon muttered. He'd find out what happened with Keith later. He had other business to take care of first. He descended the stairs with a single step and followed the trail to the tree line.

CHAPTER 19

Rick paused as a sharp crack echoed through the air. For a moment, he stood frozen, listening for other sounds. Simon could sense the wheels turning in his mind. The ego was billowing within him. The Louisville detective, who had over a thousand arrests in his record, was reemerging through the shell of a somewhat husky county deputy.

"Maybe we should hold back," Simon said.

His words meant nothing. Rick hustled through the woods, splashing snow with each step. The moment the gunshot echo entered his ears, his ego exploded. If he had an opportunity to get the bastards that killed Eddie, then he would do it. Simon struggled to follow him. "Rick, you said we'd hold back and observe!"

"Shh!" Rick said.

"Don't give me that 'shush' shit! You're the one who got us into this mess, and now you're making it worse."

"Something might be going down," Rick said.

"You're not a hero cop anymore, Rick!" Simon grunted. "You're a small town deputy like me. Wait for backup to get here. Like *you* said!"

Rick ignored him and pressed on. Veering to the left, he could see an opening through the woods. There was a clearing up ahead, likely the front lawn of the property. Then came sounds of heavy breathing and running feet. Rick stopped, waved a hand back to Simon, signaling for him to do the same. His eyes panned the woods until finally he saw the two running figures approaching. It was a man and a woman. In the man's hand was a 12-guage shotgun. Rick pointed his Glock.

"Freeze!"

Vivian was in the process of looking back for Dillon when Jeff's hand grabbed her by the shoulder and forced her to a stop. It took a moment for the cop's voice to register. She stared ahead in stunned silence. Two deputies, wearing black winter coats, were pointing pistols at her and Jeff. Her mind swirled with numerous questions: Where'd they come from? How did they know they were here? Why are they here? Do they know about the bank?

"Wait, we didn't…" Vivian stopped speaking, not sure exactly what to say. Meanwhile, Jeff slowly lowered his weapons, holding one hand over his head to maintain a non-threatening posture.

"There's two others, one of them has a bad attitude," Jeff warned.

"Shut up and put the weapons down," Rick said. Jeff already had the shotgun in the snow.

"Listen, he's coming," Jeff said. "He's armed with a nine-millimeter. I don't think he's gonna cooperate with your orders."

"Stop talking and take the six-shooter off," Rick continued. Jeff complied and put his hands around his head. Rick glanced back at his partner. "Deputy Mayer. Place cuffs on them. Start with the male suspect."

Simon gradually moved in on Jeff. He was shaking with adrenaline, which showed in the quivering motion of his muzzle; something that Jeff noticed.

"You mind pointing that away before we have an accident?"

"Shut up, cop-killer! Turn your back!" Simon said.

"Wait, no, we didn't do that," Vivian said.

"Hands up, Missy," Rick shouted. Vivian started to speak, then raised her hands slowly. The cuff of her sleeve fell a couple of inches, revealing the black ink on her wrist. Both Rick and Simon's eyes went wide.

"Holy shit, Rick," Simon said. "You were right! This is them!"

"We have nothing to do with the killing of that cop," Jeff said. "I didn't even know about it until recently. I'm just the driver. We were gonna alert you…"

"A little too late for sweet-talking." Rick said. "Like my partner said, turn your back."

Jeff's heart raced. His instinct screamed in his brain to attempt to disarm. But these were not enemy combatants, these were officers of the law. He turned around with his hands clasped behind his head. Simon moved closer, reaching for his cuffs with one hand.

"What'd you do with our partner's body?" he growled.

"Partner? Who?" Vivian asked.

"Quit playing dumb. We saw your pal, blood-soaked, running with an axe! You chop him up? Have yourselves a cop killing ritual?"

Jeff and Vivian shared a glance. The same thought raced in their minds.

What happened at that log pile?

Jeff looked ahead. There was movement between the trees. A figure approached, holding an axe in one hand and a pistol in the other. Jeff watched Dillon's expression as he locked eyes with him. The guy was so dead-set on killing him, he didn't even notice the officers behind him. Jeff watched the Glock point in his direction.

Simon was now a meter away. The cuff links rattled as they came free from his belt.

"Hold still," the deputy said.

Jeff launched himself backward, colliding into him. He hunched low, allowing Simon's gun arm to come over his shoulder. He launched an elbow into the cop's armpit, then grabbed his gun-arm with both hands. With a twist of his hips, he threw Simon over his shoulder.

Rick adjusted his aim, ready to fire. Before his finger could complete the squeeze, a series of gunshots rang out. He crouched low and watched the woods. At that moment, there was another loud crack. At the exact same time, he felt a hard blow against the right breast of his vest, which drove him back.

As soon as Dillon saw the cops, his priorities changed. While he still wanted vengeance on Jeff and Vivian, the goal was to kill these officers before they could arrest him.

"I see you brought the cops here!" he yelled. He moved to the side for a better view of Jeff.

Jeff twisted the pistol from the struggling deputy, then aimed it back at Dillon. The gang leader saw the muzzle point at him. Dropping the axe, he darted back for the cabin, firing a few shots blindly over his shoulder. Jeff squeezed off a few rounds at him, which hit nothing but tree trunks.

"Shit!" he yelled. He looked back at Rick, who was lying flat on his back with a hand on his chest. He looked down at Simon, who was lying in a stiff posture beneath him. He watched the woods where the crazed gunman ran, then back up at Jeff. "Listen, Officer, *that's* the guy you want!" He held the pistol by its frame and extended it back down to him. Simon stared, confused, then accepted the gun back. As he stood up, Jeff hustled back to Rick and knelt beside him. "How badly you hurt?"

"Caught me in the vest," Rick said. He looked Jeff in the eye. "Can't say you didn't warn us."

"Listen, I don't know about your deceased deputy, sir," Jeff explained, "but I can tell you this: he's the guy that killed the bank manager and officer back in Richardson. And he'll kill you and anyone who comes near him. I don't believe he's mentally stable."

"How many are with him?" Simon asked.

"There's Matt and..." Jeff looked back at Vivian. "Where was Keith?"

"I never saw him," Vivian said. "But Matt...Matt was covered in all that blood."

"Some kind of internal conflict going on in your group?"

"Between us and Dillon, yeah," Jeff said. "But there's been other weird things happening around here. I don't suppose you guys were stalking our cabin all night and sabotaged our generator?"

"No, that wasn't us," Rick said. "We'll worry about those details later."

"Any idea where he went?" Simon asked.

"Back to our cabin, most likely," Jeff said. "I can assure you he won't be there long though. He's crazy and determined, but not stupid. He knows there'll be more cops coming. He's probably gonna pack up a couple things and make a run for it."

"Does he have a vehicle?"

"My SUV's still there, though there's a fallen tree blocking the path."

Rick stood up, his chest throbbing.

"What are your names?"

"Jeff and Vivian," Jeff answered.

"Deputy Rick Beck and Deputy Simon Mayer," Rick responded. "Listen, you want to earn our trust further, then stay here. Don't go anywhere. Simon and I will try and set a perimeter around your cabin. We need eyes on the suspect until back-up arrives."

"You want us to stand here in the cold?" Vivian asked.

"Sorry, ma'am," Rick said. "Back-up should be arriving soon. We'll have someone take you back to the station. You'll probably be arrested, but I might be kind enough to offer testimony in your favor. In the meantime, you'll have to wait here." He looked down at the fallen firearms. "Mind if I borrow this shotgun?"

"It's all yours," Jeff said. "It's loaded and ready to go."

"Appreciate it." Rick picked it up and checked it, then tucked the revolver into a spare holster in his vest. Despite his newfound faith in the stranger, he wasn't going to let a suspect loose in the woods with a loaded gun.

"You ready?" Simon asked.

"Yep. Let's go."
Both cops darted into the woods, following the trail left by Dillon.

CHAPTER 20

"What are you doing, man?" Matt whimpered as Dillon raced up the stairs. A moment later, he was hustling back down with Matt and Keith's duffle bags full of money.

"Went through all this for a good payday. I'm not losing all this cash."

"Even *you* won't manage to carry all of that," Matt said.

"That's why you're gonna help!" Dillon shouted. He tossed a bag at Matt, toppling him backward. He came down onto the center table in the living room, knocking it to its side. "Oh, for chrissake!"

Matt crawled to his feet.

"If the cops are here like you say, then we're screwed! We're not getting anywhere!"

"Fine! You can wait for them here," Dillon said, snatching the bag back. "Or, you can come with me. Your choice!" Matt stared at the money bags, then at the woods outside. One thing was for sure, he didn't want to remain here for another second.

"How are we gonna get out?!" Matt said. Dillon dangled the SUV keys taken from Jeff's bedroom. "But the tree?"

Dillon thought for a moment. For once, the drunkard offered a decent point. It would take too long to carve out a portion of the blockage wide enough for the SUV.

"How frozen is that ice?" Dillon asked.

"I don't know. Frozen. Why?"

"That other cabin is along the shore a mile or two down. We can drive down the shoreline without getting stuck, and then come out on the beach of that other property."

"The shoreline isn't all beach," Matt said. "Some of it is steep drop-off. We'll be in the water entirely."

"Then that ice better hold! Come on! We can't wait." Matt followed Dillon outside. The sight of the woods caused Matt to slow down. He looked back and forth. Somewhere, that thing was lurking. Dillon immediately loaded the money into the SUV then glanced back up at him. "Dude, I've about had enough of your foolishness. Get down here now before I lose my shit."

"Dillon," Matt stammered. "That thing was back that way…"

"Oh, great, you're talking about a *thing* again," Dillon grumbled. He glared at the blood on Matt's coat. "Fuck, you had a mental breakdown and killed Keith, didn't you?"

"What?! NO!"

Dillon's sneer turned into a smile.

"It's okay. The guy was becoming a pain in my ass. Sooner or later, he would've ratted us out to the cops. You didn't have to do it so enthusiastically, though!" He pointed to the axe, discarded by the porch step.

"I didn't kill him!" Matt pleaded. "There's a monster out there! A devil beast!"

Dillon shook his head. It appeared Matt had completely lost his marbles. There was no time to talk sense into him. The cops were coming, and he needed to get out of dodge.

"Fine. You wait here."

"Alright!" Matt croaked. He hurried down the steps and got into the passenger seat. Dillon started the engine and put the wipers to work, uncovering the windshield.

As the view cleared, he cut the wheel to the right and accelerated. The tires spun, hardly getting any traction. He put it in reverse and floored the pedal. The SUV went back about twelve inches before getting stuck. He shifted back to forward gear and accelerated again. This time, he was able to get enough traction going.

"Finally," he said. He followed the various foot trails that led to the log pile. The snow was thick, but mashed down enough which allowed the tires not to get too jampacked. After a few moments, he had a slow steady pace going.

Rick and Simon were at the edge of the woods when they heard the engine. By the time they reached the property, the SUV was starting its path, seemingly going right for the lake.

"Where the hell's he going?" Simon asked.

"I have no idea, but we're not gonna let him get far," Rick said. He leaned against a tree and shouldered the shotgun. "Go for the tires first."

He aimed down and left, going for the front left tire, then squeezed the trigger.

The tire burst with a loud slashing sound, shaking the entire SUV.

Dillon jolted in his seat. His brain registered the sound of gunshots, along with the reverberation from a second tire explosion. He looked to the trees, seeing the two cops firing at his vehicle.

"Fucking pricks!" He pointed his Glock and squeezed the trigger, the bullets punching holes through the window and into the trees. Rick and Simon ducked behind cover, the former returning fire with another blast of his shotgun. Pellets smashed against the car door, one of them breaking through and nicking Dillon's thigh. The gang leader shrieked and cut the wheel to the right, taking it right into the opposite tree line. With the pedal floored, the SUV shot through the snow, before plowing straight into a tree. Both men hit the dashboard, leaving them dazed.

More gunshots assaulted the vehicle, popping a third tire and blowing out the rear windows.

"Hold up," Rick ordered. He dropped the shotgun, having spent all of its shells, and switched to his Glock. He took a step out from the tree line, keeping the driver's side locked between the notches of his sights. "Blessing County Sheriff's Department. You are under arrest. Come out with your hands high. If we see a firearm in your hands, we will open fire!"

There was no movement, nor was there any reply.

"Did we hit them?" Simon whispered.

"No idea. Don't take your eyes off those car doors," he said.

"We should've waited for back-up," Simon groaned.

"Knock it off and pay attention," Rick hissed. "Stay together now. We'll cover the position from right here." They slowly approached the SUV then stopped about thirty feet behind it. From where they stood, both officers could cover each side. The engine still ran, despite being crumpled against a tree. Smoke and cold air twirled from the exhaust pipe.

Inside, Dillon watched them though his mirror. Matt was shivering in his seat, on the brink of a full panic attack. Dillon noticed his hand grasping the door handle.

"Get ready to go out and shoot," Dillon said. "I'll take the one on the right. You take the other one."

"I...I don't know," Matt said.

"You have your pistol, right?"

"Yes," Matt said. He pulled it from his coat. It trembled in his hands. Dillon watched the window again. The officers continued yelling demands for their surrender.

"You ready?" Dillon said. Matt shook his head. He couldn't even think. It was as if his mind had evaporated. He stared blankly, unable to move. He sat in his seat, appearing like a corpse. Dillon groaned in frustration.

"Fine. I'll do it myself." He took a series of deep breaths, psyching himself up for his last stand. Matt continued staring into the woods. Then, suddenly, his eyes caught motion. It wasn't the wind moving the trees. It was lower, moving under its own will. It passed between the wooden bodies.

Finally, it emerged, several dozen feet in front of him, staring at him with hideous eyes. He could see the mandibles clicking together, the elongated claws outstretched at its sides, ready to impale him like it did Keith.

Matt yelled in terror, shocking the gang leader beside him.

"MONSTER! THERE!"

"Jesus, Matt! What the hell are you—"

Still screaming, Matt swung the door open and burst out into the snow, arms waving high with his pistol in hand.

"Gun! Gun! Gun!" Rick shouted. Both officers aimed at the crazed thug and opened fire. Matt's screaming turned into shuddering squeals as several bullets entered his body. Two struck through his ribs, another two in his upper right shoulder, while a fifth punched through his lower abdomen. The blood-covered thug was frozen in place for a moment before falling to his knees. He tried to yell again, only resulting in blood spitting from his lips. He fell backward into the snow, red puddles forming under him.

"Suspect down," Rick announced. Simon reloaded, breathing heavily to keep himself psychologically under control.

"Holy shit. Holy shit," he muttered repeatedly.

"It's not over yet," Rick said. He raised his voice, "Driver! This is your last chance! Drop your weapon out the window and step out with your hands raised."

Dillon roared in anger. He was trapped, yet unwilling to concede defeat. He watched the mirror. The cops were approaching, moving along the passenger side. They secured Matt's firearm and walked past his twitching body. Their shadows touched the open passenger door as they stood just of his view.

He went over every tactical option in his mind. There were only three or four bullets in his magazine by now. Despite being as good a shot as he was, it was unlikely he'd be able to kill both of them, especially with them having the advantage of Kevlar. On top of it all, his left leg was messed up from the shotgun blast, meaning he would not be able to outrun them. To top it off, he was too much of a coward to put the gun in his mouth and squeeze the trigger, meaning prison was an inevitable fate.

Rick neared the open passenger seat. He nodded at his partner, who nodded back, signaling he was ready to finish the deed.

"Last chance. Drop the gun and show me your hands," Rick announced.

"Go to hell, pig," Dillon responded. Rick tensed with frustration. This stupid thug would not give up, even when cornered.

Dillon waited, watching the open doorway. He could see the second cop through the passenger window. The idiot was crouched, which left his head exposed in his field of view. Dillon grinned and thought of trying to pull off a shot. He slowly turned to his right, his wrists angling the pistol toward the intended target.

Dillon had made his choice. Prison was no option. He'd rather get his brains blown out. Yet, if by some chance he could kill these cops and get away...the time to figure that out was now.

"The hell was that?" Simon muttered.

"Not now," Rick groaned.

"In the woods! I saw someone," Simon said. "I think there's another suspect."

"Keep an eye on the task at hand," Rick said. The sternness in his voice did not register in Simon's mind. He backed off, redirecting his Glock towards the woods. Rick glanced back, "Mayer, what are you—"

Dillon leaned forward and fired a round. For the second time, Rick was caught in the vest. This time, it cracked a rib. He staggered backward in tremendous pain, firing a few rounds blindly into the dashboard. Dillon opened the driver's seat door and dove out. A few bullets flew overhead as he army crawled in the snow. Now by the engine, he propped onto his hands and knees, counted to three, then took off running. He took long strides while stomaching the pain in his thigh as best as possible.

"There!" Simon said.

"What are you waiting for? Get after him, you idiot," Rick yelled. He was still doubled over from the bullet hit to his ribs. Simon hesitated slightly, then followed the criminal. After a deep breath, Rick followed.

Dillon weaved back and forth, evading bushes and fallen branches. The woods were a deep maze that went on forever. He couldn't go on forever. He'd have to find a place to get a shot at the cops. There was a nice wide tree less than a hundred feet ahead. On each side were thick bushes, perfect to obscure the view of him, while providing ample cover.

There was no time to strategize further. He could hear the officers moving through the trees behind him. Dillon winced from the pain in his leg as he ran in a tight bend around the bushes. After a few long strides, he was behind the tree.

He stopped and locked eyes on the figure that stood behind it. Its large angular head turned in a birdlike motion. Several black eyes stared at him. Dillon froze, momentarily questioning his senses. Only when he felt its talons rip through his abdomen, did he finally realize that he wasn't seeing things, and that Matt was telling the truth.

Blood spewed from his mouth as Dillon let out a low-pitched squeal. The beast straightened its legs and raised its arm, lifting Dillon like a trophy.

Simon and Rick ran in a tight arch, only to stop in stunned silence when they caught sight of the beast. Just as Dillon did, the officers stared for a moment, questioning their senses the entire time. What they were looking at was otherworldly. Impossible. Yet, it was real.

The beast stood on two legs, jointed like those from an insect. Its feet were large, containing two claws that curved inward. Its arms were long, each appearing to have two elbows for greater range of flexibility. Its hands were comprised of three enormous razor-clawed fingers. And impaled on one of those hands was their suspect.

It stared at his face, as though fascinated by the slow death it inflicted. Its mandibles uncoiled, exposing an inner jaw with lined teeth that were similar to a canine's.

"Holy shit! Holy God!" Rick muttered. The beast turned its head and looked right at them. The mandibles extended, releasing a horrific hiss. The cops ran back for the cabin. Behind them, snow splattered under thunderous footsteps as the beast pursued, towing Dillon's still writhing body.

"Jeff, maybe we should wait here like they said," Vivian said. Jeff was running ahead of her toward the property. They had heard the exchange of gunfire, which had come to a sudden stop.

"I can't be sure what happened if I can't see anything. If Dillon killed those cops, then we're on our own," Jeff said. Moving through a maze of pines and maples, they neared the edge of the property. The shotgun was in the snow, alongside a collection of empty shells. Up ahead was the SUV, smashed up and spewing smoke. Ten feet to its right was Matt, sprawled out in the snow. They hurried over to him, keeping the shotgun in hand.

"Is he dead?" Vivian asked.

"I don't know," Jeff said. "I think he's…" Jeff jumped back as Matt came to life, his arms reaching up at him like a reanimated corpse. Blood trickled from his mouth as he gagged for air. Jeff started to apply pressure to the injuries along his abdomen.

"Viv, get a first aid kit from the cabin. Top right shelf, kitchen. Hurry!" Vivian didn't hesitate. In a few moments, she disappeared into the cabin. Jeff leaned down to Matt. He was panicking, his mouth attempting to form words. "Matt, relax. We'll get you to a hospital. You'll be fine." Matt shook his head.

"Monster! The monster from the rock wall! It's here!"

"Not now," Jeff said.

"Run," Matt groaned.

"Matt, calm down. We'll get you help. There's no mon—" A loud roar echoed from the woods. Jeff stood up with the shotgun. Without hesitating, he grabbed the spare shells from his pocket and loaded them into the weapon. There was the sound of frantic breathing and running feet.

The two cops jumped out from the woods, their eyes wide with fright.

"Run! Go!" Rick yelled. Jeff saw the figure approaching from behind them. He stepped back, his muscles tensing uncontrollably as he saw the humanoid step out from the trees.

Vivian came out of the cabin with the first aid kit, which fell from her hands once she saw the beast. It continued to carry Dillon. He was still alive, impaled on its claws, moaning for the agony to end. She put her hands to her face and screamed.

"Get in the cabin!" Jeff yelled to the cops. The beast advanced, extending its other arm. Jeff shouldered the shotgun and fired. The beast staggered back, its right shoulder ripped open. Grey blood spewed onto the snow. He fired again, hitting it in the abdomen. The creature doubled over, then fell into the snow, along with its prize.

Dillon lay next to it, clutching the claws with his hands. He twitched, unable to muster the strength to free himself. Now, he wished he had the nerve to kill himself when he had the chance in the SUV. Death was around the corner, but the bastard was taking its time with him.

He looked up at Jeff and the other officers as they gradually approached the thing.

"What the hell is it?" Rick asked.

"Maybe it's a real sasquatch," Simon muttered.

"Knock it off, you idiot," Rick said. "Those things are supposed to have fur. This...this looks more like a bug."

"Well, I'm not waiting to decide which," Jeff said. He pumped the shotgun and pressed the muzzle to the creature's head.

With a triumphant roar, it sprang to life. Both claws lashed out, the left tearing out Dillon's gut, leaving him squirming on the ground in increased pain. Jeff fell backward, his shotgun firing high. He looked to the creature as it advanced. Its shoulder and abdominal injuries were already scabbing over. The beast had an accelerated healing process. It closed the distance and raised its claws to slash down.

Bullet holes burst in its arm and neck. Rick and Simon unloaded their pistols into the beast. It backed off, protecting its head with its arms. Jeff scrambled to his feet and backed away, pumping the shotgun again. He had only three shots remaining.

"You like that!" Simon screamed. He fired another shot, hitting the creature in the leg. "If it takes enough, it'll die!" he said. He aimed for its head and fired again, striking the beast in the palm of its hand. He squeezed the trigger repeatedly, only to hear the series of *clicks*. He saw the locked slide, ejected the mag, slammed a fresh one into the handle, then took aim again.

The beast pitched forward, its mandibles hyperextended. Wet saliva splashed Simon's face, blinding him. He staggered back, firing his gun rapidly. The creature had already darted off, evading his shots. Rick fired a few rounds at it until the creature disappeared into the trees.

"Son of a bitch," he muttered.

"Deputy Mayer? You okay?" Jeff asked. Rick turned to look. His partner had dropped his pistol and had his face buried in his hands, appearing as though weeping. There was a panicked groan echoing through those gloves. Rick quickly approached and grabbed him by the shoulders.

"Simon? What's wrong?" Simon's hands came down, peeling portions of melted skin and muscle from his skull. Rick shrieked and jumped away. Simon held his hands out, pleading but unable to speak. Both eyes were gone, as well as the nose. His cheeks turned to goo and dripped from his mouth, exposing teeth and a liquified tongue. "Jesus!" Up on the porch, Vivian cried out and darted into the cabin.

Rick babbled in shock as he watched the faceless deputy stumble towards him. Finally, he hit his knees and faceplanted into the snow, dead.

"Look out!" Jeff pointed behind him. Rick didn't bother looking back. He took off in a sprint, narrowly avoiding the beast's grasp as it reemerged from the forest. Its many wounds were already nearly healed.

"We got fucking *Wolverine* here," Jeff shouted. He blasted a shot into the creature's stomach. It was slowed, but still coming. Jeff turned and followed the deputy into the cabin. Vivian was at the door.

"Come on!" she cried out.

Rick ran in past her, followed immediately by Jeff. The creature was at the foot of the steps, its claw ripping the handrail out by the roots.

Jeff slammed the door, locked it, then grabbed the heaviest piece of furniture. Rick and Vivian moved to different ends and lifted. They propped it against the door right as the creature collided. The door cracked down the center. Another couple of hits, then it would be in. With the couch in the way, only the top third of the door was exposed. Jeff waited, keeping his shotgun aimed high. Hopefully a headshot would be enough to put it down before its regeneration could save it.

"Watch the window," he said. He barely finished the sentence when the glass shattered. The creature stuck its ugly head inside and snarled. Claws grasped the frame and pulled it further in. Rick fired his pistol, striking its face. The beast cried out and withdrew back to the outdoors. Rick ran to the window, only to see the creature move further out into the lawn. "Don't bother," Jeff said. "Help me board this up."

"It won't do any good," Rick said.

"I'd rather have this boarded up than allow that thing free passage in," Jeff said. He glanced back to the creature. Its face was healing. Instead of returning for another attack, it rummaged the yard, first grabbing Simon's body by the leg and dragging him toward Dillon.

Despite the many fatal injuries, the gang leader was miraculously alive. It wasn't a blessing, as the agony he suffered was nothing like he ever thought was possible. He was without a stomach. His spine had been nicked by the claws. There were several broken ribs, as well as internal damage to other organs including his lungs. Yet, life still clung to him. The creature stood over him and stared, seemingly fascinated by this. Its mandibles clicked together, the inner jaw biting. It pointed a finger and touched the wound, causing Dillon to twitch and moan.

"Heeeelllppp," he wheezed, looking back to the cabin. Another pained groan caught the creature's attention. It was Matt. He had rolled over onto his stomach. He was propped on his elbows, trying to summon the strength to flee. Dragging its other two prizes, the creature approached. Blood smeared over the frozen landscape behind them until it was standing over Matt.

There was no curiosity with this one. The creature raised its foot over his body. It tilted its claws downwards like curling toes, then it stomped down. The claws punched through the back of Matt's skull, the weight of the foot driving his forehead into the earth.

Dillon let out a gurgled yell. The creature looked at him again, its foot smeared with Matt's blood. Its mandibles came back again, almost forming a hideous smile. It dangled an arm over his face, the three fingers pointing down at him. Its victim's terrified mumbles did nothing other than spur it on.

From the window, Rick and Jeff watched at those three claws slowly came down. Vivian looked away and covered her eyes. Despite the monster Dillon was, there was no pleasure in seeing any human go through the torture. One final scream escaped him. The claws punched down, penetrating through his eye sockets and open mouth, silencing that scream. The creature lifted its arm, holding Dillon by the face. Blood dripped down his limp body as it turned to face the cabin.

"Jesus," Jeff said. "It's showing them to us." He lifted the living room table over the window and pounded nails along the edges with his hammer. Rick watched around the corner of the frame. It waved Dillon's body like a flag.

"You think it's doing it on purpose? Psychological warfare?"

"Maybe," Jeff said. Rick assisted in nailing the table over the window. The creature disappeared into the woods, dragging its prey behind it.

"Will it be back?" Vivian asked. Jeff wanted to lie and say 'no' in hopes of calming her nerves. Unfortunately, he couldn't deny the truth.

"Yes," he said. "Let's continue boarding up the windows. I have some spare wood in the shed. We'll go out the back door and get it. Rick, you keep an eye out for that thing."

"Go out there?!"

"Better to do it while it's gone," Jeff said.

"I suppose you're right," the deputy said. He took the revolver out from his vest and extended it back to him. "I think it's safe to assume you're no cop-killer."

"No, but that thing is," Jeff said. He checked the cylinder then handed the weapon to Vivian. "You know how to shoot?"

"Yes," she said.

"Good. Hang on to this. Blow that thing's head off if it comes near you." Jeff hurried into the kitchen, into a tiny hallway which led to the back entrance. He and Rick checked the woods for a moment, then hurried to the shed. They grabbed the spare lumber they could find, then hurried back.

"Does your headquarters know about this?" Jeff asked Rick.

"They're sending everyone," Rick explained. "The whole cavalry is on its way. Unfortunately, as you've discovered on your way in, these roads are never plowed."

"Which means they've got a while before they get here," Jeff replied. "I see. Do they know what the threat is?"

"They're coming up to take down...well, you guys. I lost my long-range radio. I can't reach them with this shit," Rick pointed at his standard radio. They began nailing boards over the back door.

"They won't know what they're up against," Jeff said.

"The best we can hope for is for them to unload into the bastard. Maybe they can inflict enough damage to kill him before he regenerates," Rick said. His breath moved in little grey clouds as he spoke. Seeing it made him realize how cold it was inside. "You said it busted your generator?"

"Yes," Jeff said. He tossed another log onto the fire then proceeded to work. They both moved out into the kitchen and applied more boards to the main window.

"Why would it do that? Because it made noise?" Rick asked.

"In that case, I don't know why it waited until we arrived to do it," Jeff said. "That thing's been working all winter."

"It did it last night?"

"Yes."

"Forgive me if I sound crazy, but doesn't it seem like the bastard did it on purpose? I mean, why else would it wait all this time to bust it up?"

"How would I know? I don't even know what the damn thing is. I didn't even know it existed," Jeff said.

"It knew we needed firewood," Vivian said. "It attacked while we were separated. It learned of our presence last night when it tracked the bear. Dillon shot at it, and it learned we had weapons. Despite its healing ability, it can be hurt. It destroyed the generator, hoping to drive us out into the woods. It drove us out so it could pick one of us off."

"Meanwhile, it went hunting. And found me and my deputies," Rick sneered. "Only a mortal bastard would be so sneaky. A bunch of headshots should do it. Its skull is thick, but I doubt it's made of diamond." He hammered another board over the door. "Where'd it even come from?"

"I have no idea," Jeff said.

"That meteorite in '92?" Vivian asked.

"I don't know. It was all stories until now," Jeff said. He grabbed another board and a handful of nails. "Let's worry about that later. Right now, let's finish this up. Viv, keep watch."

"You know these boards won't keep it out," she replied.

"I know. But it makes me feel better. I'll settle for that until back-up arrives," Jeff said. He proceeded into Dillon's bedroom and started hammering away.

CHAPTER 21

Rick stood by the window, watching the outside through the narrow space between the frame and the table that covered it. The icy wind crept through and stung his eyes. Despite this, he kept watch.

They had the cabin boarded up as securely as possible with the limited resources they had. Now, all they could do was wait, and hope that the strange beast would not return before back-up. He checked his watch. It had been over seventy minutes since he notified Dispatch. In the summer, they could easily travel the long road in twenty minutes or less going at top speed.

Damn this snow. He gazed at the frozen pool of blood out on the lawn where Simon had collapsed. Rick's mind replayed that horrific image of his face melting on a loop. It was a mental anguish he would have to endure for the rest of his life, especially after dragging the two deputies along on his crusade to relive his former glories.

He sipped on a water bottle. It was the only thing available to drink. They all craved coffee in this freezing cold. All except Vivian. The last thing she needed was for caffeine to get herself even more worked up.

She was upstairs with Jeff, who had just finished boarding the bedroom windows. He placed the hammer down and took a seat beside her. She was wearing an extra sweater, and had her arms crossed over her chest.

"Help will be here any minute," Jeff reminded her.

"I know," Vivian said, shivering.

"You sure you don't want to go back downstairs where it's warmer?" It was the fifth time he asked. She took a sip from one of Matt's bourbon bottles.

"That thing will probably come through that window," she said. "Boards and tables won't stop it. It's waiting deliberately. It knows we're afraid, and it enjoys it." She took another sip. "You saw how it relished in torturing Dillon and Matt."

"Yes," Jeff said.

"Maybe that's our fate," Vivian said. "It's our punishment for the things we did."

"No," Jeff said. "It's just a freak of nature. I don't care whether it's a demon, or an alien, or some lab experiment, it's not gonna get us. We're gonna get out of here and start over."

"What if we go to jail?"

Jeff shook his head. "I think the cops have bigger things to worry about right now." They shared a kiss, which was quickly interrupted by Rick's call.

"Guys! Something moved!"

They broke off their kiss. Jeff grabbed the shotgun and revolver and ran for the door.

"Come on. Let's go downstairs," he said.

"Safer up here," Vivian said.

"Not if we have to make a run for it," Jeff said. Vivian nodded, then got up. The cold had stiffened her muscles. The thought of running outside seemed like certain death. "I don't suppose you'll mind if I smoke at this point?"

"Screw it. I'll take one too," Jeff replied. They both lit up and hurried down the steps. Rick glanced back at them briefly, then pressed his face back into the crack in the window frame.

"I should've packed the high-powered rifle," he groaned.

"Where is it?" Jeff asked.

"I don't know. I thought I saw movement beyond those trees to the right," Rick answered. With no window on the fireplace wall, Jeff hurried to the kitchen windows. "Be careful about exposing yourself. That thing spits acid."

Jeff kept only one eye peeking through the boards that covered the window. From what he could see, there was nothing. A slight creak echoed from the left side of the building. All three occupants shook nervously, the two men glancing to each other in an attempt to determine who should check. Jeff made the move. There was another creaking sound, followed by a slight scraping. There was some sort of weight pressing down on the wall.

"I think it's climbing," he whispered. Vivian took another drink, then drew on her cigarette. "Careful with that stuff."

"Sorry," she whispered. She set the bourbon down on the floor. He was right, she didn't need the alcohol dulling her senses. Right now, she was as calm as she'd ever be. She grabbed a knife from the kitchen and held it in an attack-ready stance.

The wall creaked again, the scraping now further up. The beast was definitely climbing. Not only that, but it was attempting to do it quietly. Had Rick not caught a glimpse of it, they probably wouldn't be aware of its presence.

"It must've gone around the back," Rick whispered.

"What the hell's it up to?" Jeff said. "It can't fit through the windows up there."

"Maybe it wants to burst in through the roof? Or maybe it can rip away at the windows to make them wide enough to pull itself in?"

"If it's gonna be that flamboyant, I don't know why it doesn't come in the back door? Or the front door for that matter? No matter where it tries to break in, we'd have enough time to engage it. Why waste time being so sneaky?"

"Because it *can* be killed," Vivian answered.

"We just need to hit it enough times," Jeff said. "Kill it before it can regenerate."

There was creaking from directly above. The creature was now on the roof.

"Maybe it's waiting for us to make a run for it?" Rick said. "I imagine the bastard can jump pretty far. It could spring off that roof and take anyone who goes out that door."

Jeff shook his head. "Somehow, I don't think so."

The group waited in silence for several minutes. In that time, nothing happened. No more sounds came from above. Vivian lit up another cigarette. Rick peeked outside, then checked the kitchen windows. Nothing. By the time he returned to the living room, the place was filling with smoke.

"You might wanna go easy on those," he said.

"It's only my second one," Vivian said. She suddenly noticed the room getting darker and darker. She put the cigarette out. However, the smoke continued to fill the cabin.

"Shit. The fireplace," Jeff said. He knelt by it and checked the cover. "It's down. Whatever's blocking the smoke is coming from the chimney."

"Son of a bitch," Rick said. "It's seriously trying to smoke us out. It's got a bird's eye view up there too. It'll leap down on the first person out the door. Or spit acid on them."

"So, either we stay here and suffocate, or go out there and be killed," Vivian said. Smoke swirled around the room. Jeff prodded the fire with the ash shovel to put it out. Already, the air in the living room and kitchen had turned black. Jeff coughed violently as he dumped ash on the fire, stirring grey clouds into the mixture. However, he was successful in putting out the flames.

"The air's clearer upstairs," he said, wiping his face with a handkerchief.

"I'm not going up there," Rick said. "That thing's up there and could bust in any moment..."

It was at that moment he heard a heavy thud outside of the building. As though struck by an artillery shell, the barricades imploded into the room, knocking Jeff onto the floor. The table lay over him, covering his body head-to-toe.

Vivian screamed as the creature stepped inside. Rick raised his pistol and fired a shot. The beast lashed, its claws catching him across the forehead. The deputy spun and fell, blood seeping from the gash. The creature stepped inward, ready to finish the kills. It stepped down, its feet crunching the table, and the human laying beneath it. Jeff suppressed a moan as he felt several hundred pounds of pressure come down on him. Just a little more, then the creature would snap his spine.

The creature looked up at the last human standing. Vivian held the knife ready at shoulder height, keeping the blade pointed downward. Breathing heavily, she waited for the creature to make its move. Mandibles frolicked over its mouth. It stared at her and froze. It tilted its head, studying her with interest.

It had been decades since the beast had seen a female. Many of the human species it had killed were male. The hair on this one was almost as white as the snow outside. Yet, it was young. It had only seen white hair on older specimens. A curiosity stirred in its brain. It wanted to study her, rather than feed.

For several seconds, the monster did nothing. Vivian thought of running, but the boards covering the exit would certainly delay her. Her eyes went to the floor, where Jeff was pinned. He was gritting his teeth in tremendous pain. She saw him look up at her, then point his finger toward her foot. She glanced down. The shotgun had fallen from his grasp and ended up right by her feet, pumped and ready to fire.

She knelt down and grabbed it, then fired from the hip. The force of the recoil rolled her backward. But the shot had found its mark. The beast staggered back, its hands covering its now bleeding face. With its weight off him, Jeff leapt to his feet and drew his revolver. Vivian advanced to the window, shouldered the weapon, and fired again. The creature's chest burst open. Blood splattered onto the snow.

Vivian held the empty shotgun like a club, while Jeff fired all six rounds into the creature's neck.

The creature lowered its arms, revealing its rapidly healing face. Dead tissue flaked away, while new cells formed in its place. Two of its eyes had burst, only to regain their form. Jeff backed into the kitchen, expelling the spent cartridges from the cylinder. As he grabbed fresh bullets, the creature had already come through the window again.

He saw a subtle twitch of his head, as well as vibrating motion in its mandibles. He pushed Vivian to the floor, then dove to his left. A spray of acid streaked across the living room, arching where he had stood less than a second prior. It hit the floor and sizzled, burning its way into the ground.

The creature snarled and advanced on Vivian again. Despite her assault, it was still curious about her features.

A gunshot rang out, striking it in the neck. The creature shrieked and moved in close to the stairs, where Rick and Jeff were huddled close. Rick fired another shot, then another. Nothing.

"Fuck!" he said, seeing the slide half-locked back, an empty casing stuck in the ejector port.

"Back up the steps!" Jeff shouted. Both men backtracked into the stairway as the angry beast closed the distance.

Vivian pressed her back to the kitchen wall, feeling as though her beating heart would bounce her right off it. The creature stuck its head into the stairs and cocked its arms. Its claws straightened like spears. In a moment, it would slaughter them with ease.

She sucked in a deep breath and summoned her courage. The only weapon she had was the empty shotgun.

It'll have to do, I guess. She took a step forward, grazing the bourbon. It teetered back and forth, splashing its contents. Vivian glanced at it, then at Jeff's handkerchief on the floor.

She grabbed the bottle and tucked the rag through the neck, making sure to soak the whole thing. She grabbed her cigarette lighter and sparked a flame. The bourbon-soaked hanky went ablaze.

She chucked the bottle with all her might. The glass shattered over its back, the flame spreading on contact. Fire ripped up the stairway and over the living room floor. The creature reared back, its shoulders and back aflame. It shrieked in immense pain. With its face on fire, it thrashed about blindly, smashing sections out from the walls.

Jeff and Rick moved down the upstairs hallway, unable to see past the wall of smoke that followed them. The fire was spreading quickly. Already, it had reached the top step.

"Nowhere to go except out the window!" Rick said.

"I gotta get Viv," Jeff said.

"Can't go down that way," Rick said. "She'll have to get out herself." Jeff held fast for a moment, then finally accepted that Rick was right. They ran for the master bedroom and started peeling the boards from the window.

Vivian coughed as smoke filled her lungs. She stumbled for the open window; hands outstretched to help her find her way.

Heavy footsteps split the floorboards behind her. She looked back and saw the creature stampeding for the window. It plowed into her, launching her through the window and into the snow. The creature landed less than a yard away. It tore into the snow with its claws, extinguishing the flames on its body. It flailed for several seconds until it finally settled on its side.

Vivian brushed the snow from her eyes. The creature rested motionless, smoke twirling from its back. She slowly stood up, her eyes fixed on the abomination. She wondered if it was dead. She *hoped* it was dead. She wanted nothing but for the nightmare to be over.

The beast arose, its mouth flaring with scorched mandibles. It spotted Vivian and sprang. Its fingers wrapped tightly around her neck. She gasped and pulled at its leathery skin, unable to outmuscle its superior strength. The creature stared at her. Its skin had turned a pinkish-grey, which was fading back to its natural grey pigment. It looked to the cabin for signs of the other two humans. The fire was spreading rapidly, filling the upstairs with smoke. The whole front was nearly ablaze. It would not risk permanent injury in pursuing them. It looked back to the female. Her head had slumped to the side. It loosened its grip. She was still breathing, but had lost consciousness. The creature lifted her with both hands and ran off into the woods.

Jeff ripped the last board free and shattered the window. He stuck his head outside and saw the insectoid thing carrying Vivian into the woods.

"No, you piece of—"

"Stop—" Rick's protest was interrupted with a cough. The entire room had filled with smoke. "Get out. Now!" Jeff climbed through the window, then lowered himself for a steady landing. He let go and descended the twelve-foot fall. Rick came down right after him.

"It got her," Jeff said. "It took Vivian into the woods."

"I know. I saw it too," Rick said. "I'm sorry man. I'm really sorry. She's gone."

"No...she's not," Jeff said. He found the spot in the snow where Matt went down. A few feet nearby was the Glock he had carried. Jeff picked it up, checked the magazine, then trekked across the lawn and found Simon's Glock. He gave it to Rick, who looked at it with sullen eyes before accepting it.

"What are you gonna do?"

"I'm going after it," Jeff answered.

"You insane? You don't have enough ammo. It'll heal before you can inflict enough damage," Rick said.

"Then I'll just have to pray for a lucky hit," Jeff said.

"Jeff, we're lucky not to be dead already," Rick said. "You go after that thing, you'll be torn apart. Literally."

"You can stay if you want. I'm not leaving her behind," Jeff said. He opened the SUV passenger door in search of any weapons and ammo. The bags of money had opened, their contents scattered over the seat. Below were a couple of bottles of Matt's bourbon. "Viv might've found its weakness. It can't stand fire." He grabbed the bottles and dumped out the contents.

"What are you doing?" Rick said.

"Alcohol burns but it won't hold a flame for as long as I might need it to," Jeff said.

"Worked pretty well in there," Rick said, pointing at the burning cabin.

"I don't think I'll have the luxury of finding the creature inside a wooden cabin with carpet and furniture," Jeff replied. He hurried to his storage shed and found a hose, then brought it back to the SUV. He siphoned the gas and filled both bottles, then found Dillon's bag of spare clothing. He tore a few sheets and stuffed them down the neck of each bottle, forming Molotov cocktails.

The deputy grew increasingly anxious as he watched Jeff prepare for his crusade.

"Just hang on," Rick said. "Let's wait for back-up to get here. Once we have more people and more guns, we'll be in better shape to go after it."

"Yeah?" Jeff didn't even look at him. "How much longer will they be? Vivian doesn't have the luxury of time." He holstered the revolver in favor of the Glock, tested his cigarette lighter, then started to follow the creature's prints.

"They could be any minute," Rick said.

'Any minute' wasn't good enough for Jeff, who said nothing as he began marching into the woods. Rick winced in frustration, watching Jeff step into the array of trees. He looked back to the road, hoping to see signs of his fellow deputies.

His mind debated with itself. Something in his head knew that Vivian was still alive. But for how long? He had watched his partner die horribly. If he went after the beast, he would likely suffer the same fate. He wondered if it was even killable.

He glanced at his prized medal from his service in Louisville. The words *Awarded for Valor* were engraved over the angel wings. He recalled the feelings that came with being awarded that medal. And none of them had to do with a sense of duty. With the award came a pay rise and a promotion. There was positive media attention and a promise of a flourishing career that might even take him all the way to the rank of Captain. Then, in the blink of an eye, he lost it all. All because of a hunch.

It was a hunch that led him and his friends into Circle Mountain. *Perhaps I can make one good thing come from this*, he thought. He grabbed his standard radio.

"Deputy Beck to Sheriff Glynn?" There was no response. "Damn it. All right, Jeff. I'll come with you. Do we have any idea where it's headed?"

"Matt said something about it coming from the rock wall," Jeff answered. "There's one over here along the side of a hill. Looks like a small cliff. Maybe the thing has a lair over there."

"God, this is crazy. We're gonna get killed."

"Like I said, you can wait here for back-up," Jeff said.

"Believe me, I wish my conscience would let me do that."

CHAPTER 22

Vivian woke up to a world of darkness. For a moment, she thought she was dead until she heard the echo of her gasp. It carried on far away, as though traveling in a portal. She was on her back. She sat up and immediately checked herself for injuries. There was no blood, nor was there pain aside from a crick in her neck and shoulder. Unable to see, she felt her surroundings with her fingers. She was lying on some kind of rock. It was on a downward incline. There was an eerie whistle coming from somewhere in the distance. She held her breath and listened. It was the wind. Somewhere, it had entered this horrible dungeon and was swirling about.

If there was an opening, there was a way out.

She needed a light. The area was pitch black. If only that bastard Dillon hadn't taken her phone. Vivian reached into her pockets and found her lighter. She sparked a flame, which generated an orange glow that stretched for just a couple of feet. The flame danced like a firefly as she waved it back and forth in an attempt to get a visual of her surroundings.

There was a rock wall behind her, jagged with several pointed fragments. She was in a cave. She stood up and hit her head on the ceiling. It was an inch shorter than her. Her brain finally registered the smell in the place. It was rotten; the worst thing ever. The stench of a hundred corpses had filled this forsaken tunnel and were trapped with no outlet. Vivian fought to keep from vomiting. She hunched over, gagged a couple of times, then tucked her face under her jacket, which filtered the smell somewhat.

Finally, after regaining control of her composure, she glanced around again, waving the flame. The creature was nowhere to be seen. She wondered if it was in the cave, or had gone out to hunt some more.

At that moment, she thought of Jeff. Was he alive? Did it go back for him? Then came the ultimate questions: Why was she alive? Why did it bring her to this place? Where was she?

Time to figure that out later.

Vivian listened to the wind again. It seemed to be coming in from somewhere to the right. She kept close to the wall and slowly worked her way up the incline.

She placed one foot ahead of the other. Initially, she waited several seconds' pause between each step, afraid she'd alert whatever else was in this cave with her. So far, there was nothing, except for that haunting whistle and dreadful smell. She kept going, despite the tension in her stomach.

Stones and twigs grinded under her boots. The lighter warmed her thumb as she kept the button pressed. Soon, it would be too hot. She needed something else to use as a light; something to build a torch. She knelt to the ground and held her lighter low. There were a few twigs, most of them too short and thin. She crawled ahead and reached with her other hand, checking for anything she could use.

Her hand found something solid. It was hard as rock and as dry as though it had been in the desert. Whatever it was, it was out of reach of the glow of her flame. Vivian pulled it toward her. There was weight behind it, not from the object itself, but from whatever it was attached to. She felt like she was tugging on the arm of a large branch. Perhaps that's what it was. After all, there was other wooden debris in this cave.

Vivian gave it a hard yank and brought it into view. Her scream echoed through the cave tunnel after gazing into the empty eye sockets of a skull. She had been pulling on the bones of a limb.

She fell back, hitting her head against the wall. Dazed momentarily, she slid down into a sitting position, losing her flame in the process. Darkness swallowed her. Despite the freezing cold, she was sweating. Every breath drew that horrible odor into her lungs. She knew what it was now: the smell of countless rotting corpses that had met their end here in this cave.

She tucked her head in her arms and gave in to the tears. For five minutes, she cried in the dark, all the while cursing God for letting her survive to be alone in this dungeon. She begged for anything to take her out of this misery: a heart attack; a stroke; ANYTHING. She just wanted to die before she had to look at those horrendous mandibles again.

But alas, it did not. Vivian whipped the tears from her face and leaned back against the wall, her arms wrapped around her knees. Logic gradually returned to her. The only way to survive was to rely on herself. Perhaps she wouldn't make it out; maybe that thing was waiting for her further down the tunnel. Regardless, if there was any chance of escaping this hell, she would do it.

"Not dying here. Not gonna rot in this place," she muttered to herself. She sparked a new flame and examined the skeleton again. It was a coyote, or something in the dog family. She looked to the appendage she had mistaken for a branch. It was one of the front legs. The left one seemed to be loose at the knee, probably a result of the struggle preceding its death. Perhaps in death, this long-gone canine would assist her in life. She put both feet against the skeletal torso and pulled on the leg with both arms, once again sacrificing her flame. Her jaw clenched from the sounds of bone coming apart. She heard a sickening 'splitting' sound, then finally, the forelimb detached completely.

She lit the lighter again and examined the bone. It was about a foot long; sufficient enough to use as a torch. She forced herself to not stare at the paw. Luckily, she needed something to burn, which would cover it. She pulled up on her sweater, revealing the bottom of the tank top beneath it. She found a weak point and pulled, tearing a long sheet of it away, then tied it around the paw. She held the flame to it, and after a few minutes, she had a fully lit torch.

A bright flickering light bounced far into the cave, bringing the other wall into view. She remained crouched, making sure not to bump her head again, then looked into the tunnel. There were other skeletons from various species scattered about. To the left, she saw what appeared to be a deer. Right across from it was a pile of bones that appeared to be from a mix of various species.

Then, she saw something else. It was fabric; flannel by the looks of it. It had been torn up and cast aside. Across from it was the human it had previously belonged to. He had been stripped down to the skull. There were no arms, and several of the ribs had been broken free. Even the lower jaw had been ripped off.

Vivian coughed, then dry heaved.

Focus returned. She listened to the wind. The exit was somewhere ahead. She held the torch in an outstretched arm and slowly advanced in the dark tunnel.

CHAPTER 23

Jeff ran several yards ahead of Rick, who stopped every few-dozen feet to make sure the creature was nowhere around. High above the trees, they could see the trail of smoke behind them. Up ahead was a series of the oddly-shaped footprints which they now recognized as the creature's. There was no blood, suggesting that Vivian was most likely still alive when brought to this point. He followed the tracks between a series of trees, until finally he came to a large spacing. Beyond that spacing was the rock wall.

"Holy shit," Jeff said. Rick caught up with him and gazed at the cave entrance.

"Was that always there?"

"I can't say for sure. I never explored this area much," Jeff said. They saw the series of skeletons that littered the ground all around it. "One thing's for sure: we found where this thing's been hiding the whole time."

"You think it took your girl in there?"

"Tracks lead up to it," Jeff said. Rick's radio buzzed, making both of them jump. Rick lifted the microphone to his mouth.

"Sheriff?"

"Depu—Beck! Where the hell y—been? We've been try-- ...get in touch with you for---"

"Sheriff, what's your location?"

"ETA five minutes."

"You took the right at the fork?"

"Affirmative."

"Oh, thank God," Rick muttered. He then kicked a tree in frustration. "If only this call came in ten minutes ago."

"Go," Jeff said. "Go back and get them."

"What about you?"

"I'm going in there to get Viv. Get those guys here quick in the meantime. You know the trail. Just follow our tracks."

"It's just..." Rick sighed. "I'm not sure what to tell them. If I tell them there's some multi-eyed, acid spitting, insect-man-thing out here, they'll think I'm nuts. It'll be a half-hour before I even convince them to come out this way."

"You'll figure it out," Jeff said. "Now go! Hurry up! But first, give me your flashlight."

Rick tossed it to him, then spun on his heel and ran back to the cabin. Already, he felt his lungs burning inside his chest. Years of patrolling nonchalantly down country roads with little exercise in-between had taken a toll on him. He pushed himself to his limit while attempting to speak into his radio.

"Sheriff...you'll arrive at a fallen tree. Park the vehicles and move across the lawn. You'll find tracks," he paused for a breath, "going... into the forest. Follow them immediately. As fast...as...you can. Hurry. The situation...is...dire."

"What's going on? What's your status?"

"Bring every weapon you can carry," Rick said, ignoring the question. "I'm on my way back to you."

With the Glock in one hand and the flashlight in the other, Jeff approached the cave. He stood just outside the edge, then peeked around the corner. He held his arms crossed at the wrists, keeping the gun over the light, which was held reverse-style, keeping the beam shining straight ahead. The cave went deep into the mountainside, descending down the further it went in.

He entered, ready to watch for the beast. The Molotov cocktails were tucked in his coat pocket, the rags soaked in fuel and ready to ignite. In his pants pocket was the cigarette lighter. He would need to act fast in igniting the bottle if the creature should appear.

Jeff increased his pace, quickly coming out of the sun's reach. The smell of death hit his nostrils. He had smelled it before, but only in a much warmer environment.

In moments, he was a hundred feet into the tunnel. Suddenly, he realized he was looking at a wall of rock. At first, he thought he found a dead end. He panned the flashlight, then realized the tunnel continued to the right. It reminded him of a hallway juncture. He peeked around the corner, his finger resting on the trigger. The creature was nowhere to be seen. The tunnel descended further into the earth. No longer did it make him think of building hallways, but photos of underground tunnels used by the Vietcong during the Vietnam War. Worse, it made him think of the tunnels used by insurgents in the Middle East.

"Seems I can never escape this shit," he mumbled. He continued into the tunnel with a finger resting on the trigger. After only a few feet in, he no longer felt the wind at his back. Now, the only reminder of its existence was a loud drone that echoed through the cavern ahead.

Rick arrived at the cabin, which had become an enormous fireball. The breeze carried the smoke high over the trees and the lake, where it formed a black line in the sky for over a mile.

Sheriff Warren Glynn had stepped over the fallen tree then hurried onto the front lawn. Twenty police officers followed him, each awed by the sight of the burning building.

The Sheriff spotted Rick approaching.

"Jesus, Beck! What the hell's going on?"

"No time to explain," Rick said, panting between each word. He was covered in sweat, which glistened from the orange glow. "Like I said, we need to follow the tracks this way."

"Wait-wait-wait," Warren said. "We need a quick debriefing! Where are the suspects? Where's Deputy Mayer?"

"Where's Eddie's body?" another said.

"They're both dead," Rick said.

"Dead?!"

"Simon's dead too?" another deputy asked.

Warren's expression became hard. "I warned you to stay away until we arrived!"

"No, Sheriff! It wasn't the suspects! They're…they're all dead." The group of deputies glanced back at each other. Murmurs of confusion began to fill the air.

"What's going on?" one asked.

"Why's this place on fire?"

"Maybe we should let the State handle this."

"Alright, KNOCK IT OFF!" Warren shouted. The group fell into an uneasy silence. Warren stared into Rick's eyes. "Give it to me straight. What. Happened?"

"There's something…an animal! There's some kind of large animal in these woods," Rick said. "It's not a bear, or like anything I've ever seen before. All I'll say is that it's incredibly dangerous. It killed Simon and Eddie. Killed the murder suspects from Richardson. Trapped me in this house until it broke in, then grabbed the girl and escaped. We found its lair, and we believe it has a victim inside that might still be alive."

"*We*? What girl? I thought you said all the suspects were dead," Warren said. "Who's we? You and who else?"

"Just..." Rick stammered, already forgetting that Vivian and Jeff were part of the robbery crew, even though it was evident that they wanted nothing to do with it. *Fuck it, I'll just leave them off the hook. The suspect who did the killings is dead anyway. Bank money's recovered in the SUV. What's arresting them gonna change?*

"Just vacationers who own this cabin. Can we quit this bullshit?!" Rick shouted. "We don't have time. Whatever this thing is, we need to kill it before it murders someone else!" Rick turned and gestured for them to follow him. "This way! Come on!"

"Not until we get a clear understanding of what we're hunting," Warren said.

Rick shut his eyes and wrinkled his nose, his fingers curling into his palms. *Oh God. Here goes nothing.*

"I don't know what to call it. It's humanoid, but has insect characteristics. We shot it, but it can heal almost instantaneously. It stands eight feet tall, has claws as long as my fucking forearm! It spits acid! And..." He stopped after seeing Warren's expression, as well as those from the other cops. It was just as he expected. They looked at him like he was a maniac. Some even looked like they were about to laugh.

Warren shook his head then looked back to a deputy standing behind the tree.

"Take him back to the station. Call Dr. Goetz and tell him to come in." Warren looked at Rick. "Go with him, Deputy. We'll take care of...whatever took place here."

Rick had had enough. Not only did they think he was a lunatic, they were TREATING him as such! His hands lashed out, grabbed the Sheriff by the jacket and yanked him close.

"Have Dr. Goetz check *this!*" He thrust an elbow into Warren's chin. The sheriff fell on his back, his lip bleeding profusely.

"You son of a—" He went for his revolver, only to be hit with a kick to the chest. Rick grabbed the weapon from his holster and backed away. The cops spread out, with several of them standing ready to draw their guns. Now the situation had gotten extremely unprecedented. They had gone from standard uneventful patrols, to being called for a possible stand-off, to learning that two of their men were dead, and now being in an active stand-off...with one of their own, moments after listening to a story about an insect-man.

"Hey man," one deputy said. "Try and calm—"

Rick fired a shot into the air, shutting him up. It was then he realized he would have no problem leading the cops to the cave. All he had to do was turn and run. He tossed the revolver aside and took off running.

Warren sprang for the weapon, grabbed it, then was on his feet within the next moment.

"Get after him!" he said.

All at once, the band of cops took off running like soldiers charging an enemy fortress, while a few ran back for the vehicles to board the police snowmobiles. They turned and sped into the forest and gradually veered left, carefully maneuvering around the fallen tree and the many others that still stood.

Rick could hear the engines over the various shouts. He had minutes before he would be caught.

"Son of a bitch," he groaned. "I've made myself into a fucking suspect!" *This was NOT how I expected my day to go!*

CHAPTER 24

The minutes seemed to last forever, as did the tunnel Vivian walked in. Her knees were starting to ache from being bent, and her lower back was causing her additional misery. The flame formed a flickering ball at the end of the torch. Its light glimmered along the walls, traveling far into the abyss she traveled within.

The tunnel went for another hundred feet or so when the light found the cracks of another opening. Vivian glanced between it and the dead-end of the current pathway. There were openings on both sides. She checked the one to her right. It appeared to lead to a sharp incline which went deeper underground. She checked the opposite entrance, which appeared to continue on straight.

She trembled. She felt as though she was trapped in some kind of anthill. She wondered how deep this strange series of tunnels went. One thing was for sure: it wasn't a natural formation. The light on the walls revealed broken rock, whose fragments still remained on the floor. There were signs of charring, as if a massive fire had once swept through this place. The floor seemed strangely 'smooth' in various places. Not smooth like a sheet of glass, but not as rough as she expected a rock floor would be. It didn't appear as though dug out with mandibles or claws. Rather, it appeared burnt.

No, not burnt...

Melted.

Vivian swallowed, her mind replaying the horrific image of the creature spitting saliva. She glanced around at the surrounding tunnels, imagining how far and wide this strange habitat went.

She shivered. There was a presence in the air. She felt she was being watched. She couldn't see any movement, but it didn't comfort her any. She didn't want to wait any longer. She gave each entrance a final look to decide which way to go.

Better straight than to go deeper.

She went into the left tunnel, which curved to the right. The smell worsened, causing Vivian to slow her pace. Her hand trembled, causing burned flakes of fabric to shake loose from the torch. She proceeded further in. The air was thick. Wet. She stopped, held her breath, then proceeded through the bend. After ten slow steps, she could see the other side.

Beyond the tunnel was a large spacing. She couldn't help but think of it as a 'room'. The ceiling was still low, but the walls were spaced at least twenty feet apart. In the center were rock pillars, left in place to keep the ceiling stable. The orange glow added to the hellish appearance. She passed the first pillar, bumping another skeleton with her foot. It was wet. Fresher than the ones that she had passed prior.

Beyond it was a mixture of dry and wet blood. It smeared the floor of the chamber, as though the creature had used it to paint its fortress. She backed away, only to step on the limb from another skeleton. She turned around and shrieked.

It was not a skeleton. It was Dillon, staring back up at her with empty eye sockets. His face was red, his mouth hyperextended, the teeth ripped free. She only recognized him from his sweater and hair color. His stomach still bled, though the blood was in the process of thickening. His hand was outstretched and locked in a crooked position, as though he was still attempting to grope her in death.

Vivian looked away and walked to the other end of the strange chamber, then stopped. There wasn't an exit. She waved the torch along the wall, then walked from one end to the other. She was CONVINCED she simply missed it due to the darkness. But no, there was no other tunnel.

Is this place a dead end? A place for the thing to store its kill and dine whenever hungry?

Her heart pounded. Panic was slowly creeping into her brain. Following instinct, she drew in a deep breath to calm herself. The horrible smell filled her nose, only reminding her of the horrible situation she was trapped in.

As she held the torch ahead of her, she found herself staring at the smoke. It lifted from the flame, twisting over and over in a constant stream until it hit the ceiling, where it split and traveled horizontally. Yet, the chamber hadn't filled with smoke. In fact, the air seemed mostly clear. She was too far from the tunnel for the smoke to escape there so quickly. The smoke was going somewhere.

She looked up.

The next entrance was directly above her. It was a perfect circle, wide enough for a large person to slip through, and only a couple of feet thick. From what Vivian could see, there was another chamber on the other side. She tossed the torch up through the opening then jumped and reached as high as she could. Her fingers clasped the edge on the other side. Her faced tensed with strain as she lifted herself through the passageway. She got her elbows over, then her whole upper body. With one final pull, she was up and over. She grabbed the torch and waved it. This chamber was similar to the one below in appearance. It was a little smaller, with three rock pillars holding it together.

The fire began to die. The ball had gone from the size of a baseball to that of a grape. Vivian kneeled and tore off another large strip of clothing and tied it around the still-burning torch. The flame enlarged and stretched its light throughout the chamber.

Vivian looked ahead at the orange reflection from a dozen circular objects. They were on the ground, each the size of a nickel. Behind them was an angular head. There were several curled digits, like the legs of an upside-down spider. Vivian shrieked and jumped back, hitting one of the pillars. She hugged her back to it and waited for the creature to make its move.

There was no movement. The creature just laid, there motionless. The torch was still on the ground, illuminating its body. Vivian slowly calmed herself and studied it. At first, she thought the creature had just fallen asleep. Then she realized something. This creature was smaller. Much smaller. The one that captured her stood at least eight feet. This one was close to her size, maybe slightly bigger. Vivian braved a step forward, then another. The creature didn't move. It was on its back, its body shrunken.

Vivian grabbed the torch and held it closer. There was dried blood on the back of its head, as well as some crusted residue on the corners of its mouth. It was dead. It was hard to say how long it had been dead. It didn't appear to be dead for a long time. Then again, it was hard to tell. With a healing structure like what this species had, perhaps decomposition didn't affect them the same way.

She noticed white markings along the side of its head. At first, she thought it was snow. A closer glance made her realize the color was a physical trait. The creature's overall shape and look was similar to the one that captured her, so it had to be the same species.

A different sex, perhaps?

Vivian couldn't help but notice a few strands of her hair in her peripheral vision. Even the individual hairs were perfectly white. As white as the markings on the beast.

Was this that thing's mate. Its bride? Vivian felt sick. It had killed everyone else, but kept her alive. And now, she was starting to suspect why.

"No," she murmured. "No way. Oh, God. Please. No way in hell." She had thought being with Dillon had been her ultimate nightmare. Compared to this, she would sign over her life to him. She'd do anything but live this cruel life.

A shriek echoed through the chamber. Vivian cupped her ears and turned around. The flame shined over a hole in the side of the wall, roughly the same size as the passageway in the floor. Its dull black space was quickly filled by a twisting shape. Crawling like a malformed caterpillar, the beast made its way through the chamber. Its arms and legs bent in impossible poses, bending at its duel-elbows and knees. It cleared the passage and walked on all fours. With its horrific face and curling mandibles, it truly did look insectoid.

Vivian screamed, falling over the corpse in her attempt to back away. She looked up and saw the beast advancing, its limbs vaulting high over its body.

"No! I'm not one of your own!" she screamed. The creature kept coming, its arms touching down over the dead one. Vivian kicked her legs. "You can't! You can't!" Either the creature didn't hear what she was saying or simply didn't understand. Perhaps being alone for so many years had ravaged whatever intelligence it had. Or, maybe it was always a ravenous beast that killed its mate when it failed to produce young, and now, years later, saw Vivian as the next closest thing.

She wished for death. A heart attack. A stroke. Hell, the thing could slash her throat and be done with it! Anything but this!

The torch was by her knees. She grabbed the bone handle and pointed the flame to the creature's eyes. It hissed and scampered back a few steps, the front arms clawing wildly at the flame. She waved it back and forth to keep it at bay. Already, the flame was dying down. It would only last her a few more minutes at best.

Jeff descended into a winding tunnel, which proceeded further down into the lair. His light found all kinds of abrasions on the floor and walls, each reminiscent of claw marks. The cave was surprisingly spacious, as though intended for several lifeforms to pass through.

An echo traveled down the rock corridors, causing him to stop and listen. It was either a shriek of some kind, or a scream. Either way, there was something beneath him. He rested his finger on the trigger and proceeded down the corkscrew-shaped pathway.

After descending what he approximated to be thirty feet below ground level, he came to a large round tunnel. He nearly hesitated, as the thing had an organic look to it that made him think of the inside of a huge esophagus. Another echo came through the tunnel. This sound included words.

"NO! GET AWAY!"

Jeff sprinted through the tunnel. There were snarling sounds accompanying her words. The creature was near her. Jeff grimaced, fearing he was too late. He passed a few junctures which led to other passageways. Each time he slowed to make sure he was going the right way. The sound led him to a right hand turn, which took him fifty feet down a steep incline. He saw the flickering glow of Vivian's torch at the bottom.

Jeff grabbed one of the Molotov cocktails and lit the rag. He entered the chamber with the cocktail reared back over his shoulder. There was a brief pause, as he was taken off guard by the creature's unholy shape and posture. In front of it was Vivian, waving her torch at its face. With a whip of its claws, it struck the bone handle. It split in two, the burning end fading to black upon hitting the ground. It moved in on Vivian, rearing up on its back legs. Its lower abdomen jutted toward her. Like an appendage in itself, it began twisting into a strange posture.

Jesus, is it attempting what I think it is?

Jeff had no interest in staying long enough to find out. He beamed the flashlight onto the creature. It jerked toward him, its arms briefly covering its eyes. With a rebounding shriek, it moved away from Vivian and straightened its stance into a humanoid pose.

"Hey!" Jeff shouted. "No means no, jerkoff!" The creature bellowed, then began to charge. Jeff launched the bottle with every ounce of strength within him. It struck dead-center in its chest. Flaming gas consumed the creature, sending it into a crazed frenzy. It flipped onto its back, thrashing all four limbs into the air like tentacles.

Fire danced in the chamber like raging water. Mountains of smoke billowed, quickly filling the entire space.

Vivian sprinted to Jeff and took him by the hand.

"This way!" he said. He led her up the incline. Behind them, the creature threw itself into the mouth of the tunnel. Its face and body were heavily charred. Jeff drew his pistol and turned back. Deafening shots echoed through the tunnel, the bullets striking the beast in the face. It scurried back out of reach, stepping back into the pool of fire. Another loud screech followed.

Jeff and Vivian reached the top of the incline and looked down. The orange flickers filled the opposite end. A black shadow took shape, growing larger as the beast approached.

"My God, it just won't die," Jeff said. "Maybe the fucker can't be killed."

"It can," Vivian said.

"I don't know," Jeff said.

"No...it *can*," Vivian said. "There was a dead one in there. If that one can die...then it can die."

"Then let's hope those cops have enough lead to do the trick." Jeff took Vivian's hand and led her down the tunnel. At the end, they took a left turn. Jeff recalled the paces and landmarks he had seen on his way down. About fifty feet ahead would be the spiraling pathway.

The creature ascended the incline on all fours. Already, most of its burnt flesh had regenerated. Its claws sank into the ground and pulled it up. Still on all fours, it darted into the next tunnel.

Jeff and Vivian could hear it behind them. By the time they reached the spiraling pathway, they could see the beast emerging behind them. Vivian gasped. The beast was now climbing along the ceiling, scampering upside down toward them. As fast as they could, they hurried into the spiraling tunnel and worked their way up.

CHAPTER 25

"Deputy Beck! Stop where you are!" Sheriff Warren Glynn's voice sounded further away. Despite Rick's fatigue, he was staying far ahead of his fellow deputies. The lack of physical exertion he felt during his three years in the Sheriff's Department was far worse on his colleagues than on him. Most of these deputies were dealing with a decade or more of low-level policing, versus Rick's experience of actually chasing after criminals. That, and he was one of the few who hit the gym a couple of times a week.

Rick could see the rock cliff up ahead. Just a few hundred feet to go and he'd be there.

"Rick!" Warren yelled again. His voice was drowned out by the sounds of snowmobile engines. Rick looked over his right shoulder. One of the deputies was speeding right toward him at full speed. The guy didn't hide his snake-like grin. Rick stopped and dove back. The snowmobile splashed the snow where he had stood.

Rick lifted his face from the snow.

"You freaking psycho!" He couldn't believe it. These guys were actually trying to run him over. Rick stood up, only to dive again as the other snowmobile closed in on him. He fell into a summersault and rolled back onto his feet, splashing snow the entire way. For a moment, he had lost all sense of direction. He looked back and forth in search of the cave. By the time he spotted it, the deputies were only about fifteen feet away. The snowmobiles circled him like sharks in chum-filled water.

Rick attempted another run, going between the two snowmobiles. One of the deputies arched his vehicle to the right and followed Rick to the cave. He pulled alongside him and thrust out his boot, hitting Rick between the shoulders.

Rick fell face-first into the snow. He clawed at the ground as though climbing a mountain, crawling a couple more feet until the group of deputies converged on him. Hot breath filled the air as panting deputies grabbed Rick by the jacket and lifted him up. They twisted his arms behind his back to cuff him.

"You assholes!" Rick shouted. "Check the cave. The Cave!" "I oughta bury you in that cave," said a very angry Warren. The deputies began slinging their weapons over their shoulders and holstering their sidearms.

"You guys! Keep your weapons out! It can be everywhere." Rick's voice was frantic. Mad. Some deputies shook their head in sadness, others laughed, while a couple curious ones started moving toward the rock cliff. The sight of the cave was an interesting one to them.

"Let's catch our breath a moment and we'll get moving," Warren said to the deputies.

"Sir? Should we check out the cave?" one of the deputies asked.

"It looks pretty deep," another said. The two deputies took a couple of steps in. Warren shook his head.

"Maybe. Not this moment. I want to get organized to do that. First, I gotta see if I can convince the fire department to come out here. We'll need an arson investigation."

"You dumb fucks! Jeff and Vivian are in there!" Rick shouted.

"Did they get taken by the alien too?" Warren said. Some of the officers chuckled.

"It's not a joke!" Rick shouted. He lunged but was held back by the other deputies. "GodDAMNit, take those cuffs off me."

"We will. When we get you to the station," Warren said. "And for godsake, will you knuckleheads take his gun off him?" The deputy behind Rick responded with a dumbfounded "oh!" and reached for the holster.

"Sir?" one of the deputies by the cave said.

"What now?" Warren asked.

"I think I hear something…" The two deputies wandered a few steps deeper and beamed their flashlights. They shared a glance and nodded, confirming to the other that they could definitely hear running footsteps. But there was something else beyond that. Something moved without rhythm, gradually growing nearer along with the footsteps.

Warren, along with two other deputies, stepped into the mouth of the cave. Everyone was dead silent as they listened. They could hear it too. The Sheriff rested his hand over the grip of his revolver, then looked back at Rick.

"Tell me again what you saw?"

Jeff and Vivian shot out of the spiraling tunnel and ran down the connecting pathway. They ran several hundred feet to where it connected to the cave entrance. The creature was still on the ceiling, its mandibles outstretched. It was ten yards behind them and gaining.

"Turn here," Jeff shouted. He shoved Vivian through the somewhat narrow space and followed her out. The creature bellowed, striking the corners of the juncture with its shoulders. It angled its body, breaking rock as it came through, then moved down the side wall.

Vivian and Jeff continued until out of nowhere, they were hit by several bright beams of light. Behind those lights were several uniformed men. They converged upon the two survivors and guided them out of the cave.

"You're okay! Blessing County Sheriff's Department. I'm Sheriff Warren Glynn. We're here to—HOLY SHIT!" The deputies all erupted into panic as the creature leapt from the ceiling to the ground.

"Holy mother of Christ!" "What the hell is that?!"

Warren grabbed for his revolver. Blood spewed from his mouth as his insides imploded. The spear-like fingers penetrated his stomach and emerged out his back. The creature lifted its skewered prey off its feet. Its other hand closed around the Sheriff's head and gave an abrupt twist. Warren's body spasmed then went limp. The creature twisted back and pulled. Skin and muscle stretched then split as the head detached, a blood-splattered section of vertebrae protruding from the neck.

Deputies screamed and fled from the cave, causing their confused colleagues to advance in order to understand what happened. There was the sound of ripping and tearing before Warren's body was hurled from the entrance in various pieces. The creature emerged from the cave with a bounding leap, landing on one confused deputy. Clawed feet penetrated his torso. The creature twisted its feet, its claws acting like two giant drills ravaging the deputy's midsection.

The officers were in complete disarray. Some fled to their cars, while others drew their weapons and started firing at the beast. It jumped from its recent kill and ran in a zigzagging motion. Bullets zipped all around in a muddled crossfire. The beast weaved around a tree and found another deputy. A single slash of its claw severed his head. The smell of fresh blood filled its nostrils, emboldening it to continue the slaughter.

Another deputy fired his pistol. Overwhelmed with fright, her aim was all over the place. A stray bullet from her gun streaked by the creature's shoulder and plunged through the eye-socket of one of her fellow deputies. The unlucky cop's head jerked back, a fountain of blood spilling out from the exit wound. As he collapsed, the creature advanced onto the woman. She fired off another round. It absorbed the bullets in its chest, never slowing or showing any indication of pain. It plunged a set of fingers through her abdomen, then sliced its other claw across her neck, decapitating her.

It tossed her body aside and continued its crusade. A shotgun blast hit its shoulder. Blood and skin splattered, the force jerking the beast to its left. Another shot hit its lower midsection. A volley of nine-millimeter rounds ensued, striking its back and legs. The creature staggered and fell to one of its knees. The deputy with the shotgun felt an upsurge of confidence as he watched his shots tear into the beast. Any moment now, it would be dead. He chose to advance with intent to place a shot into its face.

He stood within a couple of yards and shouldered the shotgun.

The creature reared back, its mandibles flaring. The deputy squealed; the shotgun injuries were no longer present. It sprang at him with claws outstretched. As he tried to fire, he felt them rip into his shoulders, spinning him to the side. The finger completed its squeeze on the trigger. He never noticed the splattering of blood from his fellow deputy caught in the way of the twelve-gauge.

The beast knocked the shotgun from his hands then grabbed both his arms. It yanked outward, pulling both arms out by the roots. Blood squirted from both shoulders, the armless deputy shrieking in agony before succumbing to shock. The beast turned to the right, as two deputies lined up to blast it with high-powered rifles.

A stream of acid spurted from its jaws, encasing both of them. The effect was instantaneous. The flesh turned to jelly and fell from their bones. Their cries of agony were short-lived, as the acid burnt through their vocal cords. The sight of their skeletal corpses drove the remaining deputies into a panic. They scattered, abandoning the fight in favor of saving their own lives.

A few stray bullets zipped near Jeff and Vivian, causing them to dive into the snow. They looked up ahead, seeing the melting deputies fall to their knees, their bony hands and faces still writhing. Several feet beyond them, the creature attacked another. A single slash split the officer's belly wide open. Intestines unfolded and fell into the snow, their grotesque image quickly covered by the deputy's limp corpse.

Up ahead was Rick Beck. Like them, he was on the ground to avoid stray gunfire. His hands were still cuffed behind his back. Jeff and Vivian crawled over to him.

"You have keys?" Jeff asked.

"Yeah. Black leather pouch of my duty belt," Rick said. Jeff found the keys and uncuffed him. Rick's hands came free and immediately found his Glock, which was foolishly left on by his detainers. He stared out at the carnage, first seeing Warren's head glaring at him from the snow. Beyond it was another corpse, and another. Another scream filled his ears. The beast had found another deputy. He had fallen to his stomach and tried to crawl away. The creature grabbed him by the ankle, then spun on its heel, swinging him like a baseball bat. The deputy's head collided with a tree and imploded, ending the cries.

Rick felt numb. He had led all of these people to this lake in the middle of nowhere, only to watch them get slaughtered. In the snow beside him, his prized medallion glistened from the grey sunshine. He stared at it for several seconds, then looked back to the creature. It closed in on another deputy. She blasted it repeatedly with her rifle but it didn't stop. It slashed, severing her wrist from the grip, then drove its claws through her temple.

"My God, they didn't stand a chance," Vivian said.

"They wouldn't believe me. I had to get them to chase me up here," Rick said. He glared at his medallion again. He grabbed it and tossed it away in a fit of rage.

"Don't," Jeff said to him. He watched the deputy stand up and draw his Glock. Jeff grabbed him by the shoulders. "Rick, DON'T!"

Rick ignored him and rapidly squeezed the trigger. He wasn't sure if he hit the thing, as his eyes were fixed on the fountain of blood spewing from another deputy that it tore into.

The beast hacked the deputy with its claws, gradually cleaving him down the middle. A couple of meters ahead of it, another deputy fired a shotgun into its face. The beast lurched backward, then spat its acid saliva, drenching the officer.

Rick fired the remainder of his magazine, then watched in despair as the officer succumbed to his agonizing death. The creature waited for a moment while its injuries healed, then looked into the surrounding forest. Several officers ran toward the cabin, while the rest were dead. Only three others remained. It turned toward Jeff, Vivian, and Rick.

"Oh no," Vivian said, her voice shaky. She felt her throat tighten at the thought of being recaptured. "Jeff?!"

The creature slowly approached. Jeff took the second Molotov cocktail, lit the rag, and flung it at the beast. It hit the tree beside it and shattered, the gasoline igniting into a tidal wave of fire. The beast screamed and darted away, its leg caught in the flame.

"Let's go!" Jeff said. "Take the snowmobiles!"

"To where?" Rick said. "Can't go to the cabin. The tree's still blocking the damn road. Even if we cut through the forest, we won't outrun the bastard." Jeff guided Vivian onto one of the snowmobiles, then sat in front of her.

"The lake!"

"The lake? Jeff, I'm not sure that ice will hold!" Rick protested.

"You do what you want. I'm gonna chance it. If it holds, we can take it to Schroeder's property. From there, we can find the road and take it all the way to town." He didn't wait for any acknowledgement from the deputy. He accelerated the snowmobile to its maximum speed and veered toward the water.

No other choice, Rick thought. He sped onto the lake, carefully maneuvering between the blockade of trees between it and him.

A deafening roar overtook the forest. The beast thrashed the snow until the fire on its leg disappeared. Without waiting for its healing to complete, it began its chase. It climbed high into the trees and pursued from high above, passing from branch to branch all the way to the lake. Debris rained into the snow behind Rick, forcing him to push the snowmobile to its limits.

He looked up, unable to see the creature above him. He looked ahead.

"Fuck!"

He veered right to avoid the tree that was less than six feet ahead of him. He sideswiped the trunk, chipping wood and metal. The snowmobile shook as it continued down the hill. The exhaust spewed dark grey air.

Rick veered back and straightened his path.

Up ahead, Jeff and Vivian were on the water. The ice creaked loudly beneath them, but held firm just enough to sustain their weight. Five seconds later, Rick crossed the shoreline and blasted over the lake's snowed-over surface.

Another bellow caused him to look back.

The beast leapt from the tree. It traveled the air in a downward arch, landing less than a yard behind him. The weakened ice exploded under its weight, plunging the creature down into the icy water below.

The ice continued to split rapidly like a fault line during an earthquake. Rick shook in his seat. He heard wet splitting beneath him. A heartbeat later, gravity did the rest.

"Shit!" he shouted. He jumped to the side as the snowmobile sank into the water. He hit the ice, which was already splitting under his weight. "Shit...shit... shit..." he muttered.

"Rick's down," Vivian said. Jeff glanced back and saw the deputy struggling to not fall into the rupture.

He completed a tight circle, cracking the ice beneath them. He accelerated right for Rick. Vivian leaned to her left.

"Don't miss," Jeff said. "I'm gonna have to pull away the moment we get near him or else we'll be swimming."

Rick looked up and saw her hand outstretched. Jeff slowed the snowmobile for a single second, then started to veer right. In that moment between, Rick and Vivian's hands locked together. Rick was pulled through the snow as the ice behind him collapsed into the water.

"Jeff! Jeff!" Vivian cried. Jeff looked back. She was barely keeping her grip on Rick's hand. Aside from that, his face was red from being dragged along the snow. He slowed to a stop, allowing Rick to prop himself onto the side.

"Thanks! Let's go," Rick said.

As Jeff accelerated, the ice beneath them exploded upward, resembling a white volcanic eruption. Following it was the beast, thrashing about as it attempted to gain footing on the ice. It reached high, puncturing the hull with its claw. The snowmobile jerked as its momentum drove it away from its grasp.

The beast took its insectoid pose, reaching with all four limbs to pull itself out of the water. Its attempt backfired as its claw split the ice ledge, causing a chunk to break off. The creature thrashed angrily and started again.

"It's not gonna quit," Rick muttered. All three of them smelled gasoline. Rick glanced behind them again, this time looking at a wet line in the snow. They were leaking gas.

"We won't get far on this..." Jeff said. With no other choice, he continued speeding for the shoreline.

CHAPTER 26

The snowmobile sputtered as they neared Schroeder's property. By the time they reached the shoreline, the engine gave out.

Surprised it even lasted that long, Jeff thought as the trio disembarked. They looked out into the lake. The creature had finally lifted itself back onto the ice. Dripping wet, it marched for the shoreline, arms outstretched. It moved cautiously, gradually increasing speed as it closed within a thousand yards of the shoreline.

"Oh, God," Vivian said.

"Come on! To the cabin!" Jeff said. They raced up to the property. The propane tank was up ahead, still smashed against the tree. It was obvious now to Jeff why his tank was never filled.

"You think we can use that truck?" Vivian asked. She ran up to it and screamed when she saw the driver's charred skull. Jeff pulled him out of the seat and checked the controls. The keys were still in the ignition. He tried starting the engine, which turned over repeatedly and died.

"Damn it! Looks busted up," Jeff said.

"Keep going. I have a snowmobile around the corner," Rick said.

"How far is that?" Jeff asked.

"A couple hundred yards up the road," Rick answered. A low-pitched roar drew their attention back to the shore. The creature was only a few dozen meters out.

"We won't make it," Jeff said.

"We can't hide out in the cabin," Vivian said.

"Then let's take the pickup!" Rick said, growing increasingly determined.

"Unless the keys are in the ignition, we won't be able to start it," Jeff said.

"Fuck you. I'll hotwire the damn thing," Rick said.

"We won't outrun the thing in this snow. Not with an engine that's been static for days in five-degree weather, in twelve-inch snow. Not even with four-wheel drive."

"So, your suggestion is to stand here and wait for the damn thing?" Rick argued.

"Yes," Jeff answered.

"WHAT?" Vivian cried out.

"Let's lure it into the cabin," Jeff said. "Rick...go ahead and start that truck. Vivian, go into the cabin. There should be a back exit. Be ready to hightail it when I draw the creature inside. Once it's in, we'll block the doorway with the truck then douse the bastard with propane and have ourselves a little cookout. Fire is the weapon most likely to kill it, as long as we keep a constant flame on it."

"Jeff, I'm not sure if we can pull it off..." Rick said.

"WE CAN! We've hurt it before. Fire is our best weapon. I've seen how this thing acts. If we trap it, we can get a steady flame on the bastard and keep roasting it until it's dead. It's our only chance. If we don't do this, that thing will be on our ass all the way back to town!" Jeff leaned in and touched his forehead to Rick's like a drill sergeant. "GO!" After slight hesitation, Rick started his run for the pickup truck.

Vivian felt herself starting to freeze up. Forcing herself to power through the fear, she bolted for the cabin while Rick darted for the pickup truck. Jeff pointed the Glock at the beast.

The creature didn't rush. Its mandibles clicked and its claws curled. The beast was going to savor this kill. Jeff realized that this kill had become personal for the beast. He was the one who invaded its lair and doused it with fire. Worst of all, he *stole* its new mate. His death was to be a slow and agonizing one.

Rick reached the truck and let himself in. As expected, the keys weren't in the ignition and there was no time to search for them. He ducked down and pulled the wires out to start hotwiring. He trembled as he heard the creature bellow once more. It was as though it was trying to employ psychological warfare on them. Though he didn't want to admit it, it was working.

He touched the wires together. The engine turned over, but didn't yet spark. He peeked around the windshield and saw Jeff standing his ground, while the creature advanced.

"This isn't going to work," he said outwardly. He hurriedly touched the wires together. "Come on. Come on."

In the cabin, Vivian watched through the window as the creature came within a dozen yards of the cabin. Jeff bravely stood firm. Remembering his instructions, she hurried through the back kitchen area. A right turn led her through a small utility area, where the owner kept a few power tools and supplies. She noticed a welding torch and a separate gas cannister.

She picked them up. Luckily, they were both heavy, indicating they were full.

These might come in handy.

"Come on, you ugly prick," Jeff muttered. The beast roared back at him. He saw the subtle twitch in its neck, the very one he saw each time it spat acid. The time to act was now.

He aimed high and placed several rounds into the creature's face, briefly halting its advance. Fleshy circles exploded along its face, one popping near one of the mandibles. The creature jerked to the side, its saliva spewing out into the snow. Jeff hit repeatedly, this time aiming for its throat. Flesh exploded into thin grey strands. Out of the wounds came smoke. The creature spasmed and staggered back.

Jeff smirked. He must have hit one of the acid sacks in its throat, which was now spilling into its body. The creature writhed in agonizing pain. Then, out of nowhere, it darted for him in a crazed blitz. Jeff dove through the doorway, narrowly escaping the reach of its claws. Blinded by pain, the beast smashed along the wall to the right. It hit with the force of a charging rhino, exploding the section of wall into splinters. It lashed blindly, its claws tearing anything they could find.

It bashed the room, tearing down the entire wall separating it from the living room.

Jeff discarded the empty pistol and drew his revolver, then planted a round again in its face. The creature screamed and charged. The claws battered the wall behind him. Jeff hit the floor, once again avoiding its grip. He started to regret his plan to fight it. Not only did the beast have razor sharp claws and hot acid, it had the strength of a hundred men. And now, it was pissed! It was as though he was battling a wounded grizzly.

The creature struck the wall again, almost as though deliberately, exposing the outside air. It finally turned and gazed at its prize. It was right at its feet, ready to be skewered.

"Hey!" a voice called out. The beast looked ahead. At the back of the room stood its new mate.

Vivian unscrewed the gas can lid.

"Sorry, I'm not into you." She hurled the metal can at the creature's face. Gas spilled over its body while the can fell to its feet. Jeff scampered back on his elbows, then aimed the revolver at the can. His four remaining shots pierced the metal exterior, the last of which produced a spark large enough to ignite the fuel. The gas erupted, lighting the beast's entire frontside.

An ear-piercing shriek filled the cabin interior. The beast charged in a blind rage, smashing the wall near the stairway. Flames spread with each footstep. It smashed blindly; its entire face encased with fire.

Jeff heard a dozen dull creaking sounds from within the building.

"Oh, shit," Jeff muttered. He grabbed Vivian and shoved her out of the building as the upper floor crashed down on top of them. Flooring, rafters, walls, roofing, all broke apart into mulch.

Vivian lifted her head from the snow and looked back. The whole side of the cabin had caved in on itself, the supports having been weakened by the creature's rampage. Flames flickered high through the collapsed roof as the fire grew. Jeff was nowhere to be seen.

"Jeff?!" she yelled. She hurried to the debris and pulled a hot plank of wood out of the way, then a section of wall. "Jeff, are you alright?!" She could hear faint coughing from somewhere in the ruins.

"I've had better days," he responded, his voice muffled.

"Are you hurt?"

Under the ruins, Jeff assessed himself as best as he could. He could move his arms fine. He didn't feel any major pain in his waist or legs, other than relatively minor throbbing. He felt something pressing against his back. He tried pushing up against it, but it wouldn't budge.

What really concerned him was the intense heat he felt. The cabin was rapidly turning into one big fireball. He tried pulling himself free of the collapsed rafters, but could not budge more than a couple of inches. Large chunks of cabin were lodged together by his shoulders, keeping him from going anywhere.

"I'm pinned," he replied. "Get out of here. Don't let that bastard get you."

"No! I'm getting you out!" Vivian argued. She started rummaging through the debris, dragging pieces of roof out of the way.

Rick kept his head low as he sparked the wires together.

"Come on, you prick." He tried it again. Finally, the engine came alive. Rick breathed a sigh of relief then looked over toward Vivian. "Come on! Let's go!"

"Jeff's trapped!" she called back. Rick's face tensed. He glanced between the burning cabin and the road. Terror had him firm in its grip. The desire to flee was overpowering any sense of morality he had, or thought he had.

"Get in the truck!"

"Help me get him out!" Vivian yelled.

"We can't help him," Rick said. "Get in the truck! I'm sorry, we'll have to leave him." Vivian didn't move. Rick tensed, then shouted with blazing eyes. "Let's go. NOW!"

"What's wrong with you?!" Vivian shouted. "He came back for you. He's still alive, yet you're willing to just leave him? What kind of cop are you? I thought you guys believed in enforcing justice! Help people! Wasn't that why you came out here? Or is it all part of a quest to make a name for yourself?"

Rick didn't respond. He glanced back toward the road.

"Fuck it," he muttered. He slipped into the truck and buckled the seatbelt.

"Deputy!" Vivian cried.

"I'm sorry," Rick said. He backed the truck up, the wheels struggling to power through the compacted snow.

A resounding boom echoed from overhead. Flaming embers shot through the air like meteors as the creature erupted from the ruins. Its skin was charred, its face half melted off. Its flesh burned at a pace compatible with its healing process. Only two of its many eyes were well enough to provide vision. It saw the female backing away from the flames. Several meters to the right was the other human, who had just boarded the truck.

The creature bent its legs, then sprang. Rick screamed as its feet crashed down on the hood of the truck. Its claws punched through the windshield. His scream turned into a dull grunt as the claws punched through his ribs. It pulled him out, the glass shards scraping his skin. The beast stood on the hood and stared him in the face.

Rick spat blood, his eyes wide with pain and fright.

Vivian covered her eyes as the mandibles tore into his face, shredding his nose, cheeks, jaw, and eyes. After a moment, it looked as though his face had been through a blender. It sank its claws into its abdomen and pulled, separating his waist from his abdomen. Blood and guts fell over the truck as it raised the two halves victoriously, then tossed them aside.

The beast turned and gazed at Vivian. Its face had finally begun to heal. Two more eyes regenerated, the dead flesh falling away to make way for the fresh cells. She shuddered and backed away slowly. The creature stepped off the truck and approached.

Her eyes welled up.

No. This can't be happening.

The creature growled, its mandibles coiling over its inner jaw. Its body slowly healed, though it still trailed smoke. Its inner organs recovered from its own acid spillage.

"Get away," Vivian muttered. She grabbed a plank of wood off the ground and swung it. It split over the creature's face, who didn't even flinch. It lashed out and grabbed her by the throat. Vivian choked, dropping the plank. She pulled at the creature's arms futilely. It lifted her off the ground. Her fists struck its face and her feet kicked into its abdomen. It was like fighting a brick wall. Vivian could not outmuscle it. It released her throat in favor of wrapping its arm around her shoulders, pinning her to its chest.

"NOOO!" Vivian screamed as the other arm tightened over her back. She felt mummified in its grip. Horrid breath escaped its mouth as it began carrying her back to the lake.

Jeff rocked back and forth, unable to overpower the weight of the debris atop of him. The heat intensified with every passing second. He felt as though he was in a furnace.

He yelled in agony, unable to outmuscle the trap. His plan had worked against him. Unwilling to accept defeat, he writhed. He punched the debris in front of his face, actually knocking a few small chunks away. He lashed out again, encouraged by the small bit of progress. Another piece fell away. He could see the snow outside. He reared his arm back and went for the large plank by his shoulder.

His knuckles smashed against the four-by-four. Jeff yelled and cursed, his hand broken. He felt the orange flames building behind him and to the sides. Smoke swirled around his face, choking him.

He was in disbelief; his plan had backfired! He pushed up again, only to be weighed down by hundreds of pounds of roof.

There was movement outside. He tilted his body as best he could until he finally saw the horror outside.

"NO! NO! YOU PRICK!"

Jeff watched helplessly as the beast carried Vivian down to the shore. He shifted his body back and forth. He paused at the dull sound of something shifting behind him. Next came a crushing pain in his leg. Jeff let out a yell as parts of the cabin crunched both knees and shins.

With the pain came a mad desperate strength. He grabbed the two planks pinning his shoulders and pushed outward. Slowly, they shifted away. Jeff cried out, his muscles bruising with the impossible deed. Finally, they were nudged far enough away for him to crawl out. He clawed at the ground and pulled, escaping inch-by-inch into the snow.

He tried to use his legs, but they wouldn't respond. He could feel the wetness of his own blood spilling between his skin and jeans. Regardless, he continued to crawl out until he was nearly entombed in the thick snow.

Jeff caught his breath and lifted his head. He could barely see the beast now. It was at the shore, still carrying Vivian in its arms. Her horrified cries echoed high over the trees.

"NOOO! HELP ME!!!"

He tried to stand, but his legs were shattered.

"No!" His voice came out a weak groan. He looked around for anything to help him. The truck's engine was smashed, as was the propane tanker, and the deputy's snowmobile was hundreds of feet away. So close, yet it might as well have been on the other side of the planet.

Terror consumed him. He was in a horrible nightmare he couldn't escape. There had to be something he could do! With that terror came disbelief. He couldn't believe he failed. He was sure he had it beaten. Yet, the Creature of Lake Shadow had outsmarted him. And how, it left him to bleed in the snow; a final taunt as it walked into the distance, carrying Vivian in its arms like a newlywed bride.

Another scream traveled through the forest. Jeff could do nothing but watch as the beast turned at the shoreline, then disappeared beyond the trees, beginning its journey back to its deep dark lair.

THE END

CHECK OUT OTHER GREAT DEEP SEA THRILLERS

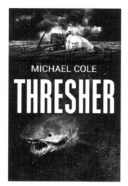

THRESHER
by Michael Cole

In the aftermath of a hurricane, a series of strange events plague the coastal waters off Florida. People go into the water and never return. Corpses of killer whales drift ashore, ravaged from enormous bite marks. A fishing trawler is found adrift, with a mysterious gash in its hull.

Transferred to the coastal town of Merit, police officer Leonard Riker uncovers the horrible reality of an enormous Thresher shark lurking off the coast. Forty feet in length, it has taken a territorial claim to the waters near the town harbor. Armed with three-inch teeth, a scythe-like caudal fin, and unmatched aggression, the beast seeks to kill anything sharing the waters.

THE GUILLOTINE
by Lucas Pederson

1,000 feet under the surface, Prehistoric Anthropologist, Ash Barrington, and his team are in the midst of a great archeological dig at the bottom of Lake Superior where they find a treasure trove of bones. Bones of dinosaurs that aren't supposed to be in this particular region. In their underwater facility, Infinity Moon, Ash and his team soon discover a series of underground tunnels. Upon exploring, they accidentally open an ice pocket, thawing the prehistoric creature trapped inside. Soon they are being attacked, the facility falling apart around them, by what Ash knows is a dunkleosteus and all those bones were from its prey. Now...Ash and his team are the prey and the creature will stop at nothing to get to them.

CHECK OUT OTHER GREAT
DEEP SEA THRILLERS

THE BREACH
by Edward J. McFadden III

A Category 4 hurricane punched a quarter mile hole in Fire Island, exposing the Great South Bay to the ferocity of the Atlantic Ocean, and the current pulled something terrible through the new breach. A monstrosity of the past mixed with the present has been disturbed and it's found its way into the sheltered waters of Long Island's southern sea.

Nate Tanner lives in Stones Throw, Long Island. A disgraced SCPD detective lieutenant put out to pasture in the marine division because of his Navy background and experience with aquatic crime scenes, Tanner is assigned to hunt the creeper in the bay. But he and his team soon discover they're the ones being hunted.

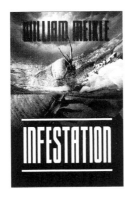

INFESTATION
by William Meikle

It was supposed to be a simple mission. A suspected Russian spy boat is in trouble in Canadian waters. Investigate and report are the orders.

But when Captain John Banks and his squad arrive, it is to find an empty vessel, and a scene of bloody mayhem.

Soon they are in a fight for their lives, for there are things in the icy seas off Baffin Island, scuttling, hungry things with a taste for human flesh.

They are swarming. And they are growing.

"Scotland's best Horror writer" - Ginger Nuts of Horror

"The premier storyteller of our time." Famous Monsters of Filmland

CHECK OUT OTHER GREAT
DEEP SEA THRILLERS

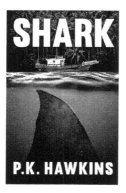

SHARK: INFESTED WATERS
by P.K. Hawkins

For Simon, the trip was supposed to be a once in a lifetime gift: a journey to the Amazon River Basin, the land that he had dreamed about visiting since he was a child. His enthusiasm for the trip may be tempered by the poor conditions of the boat and their captain leading the tour, but most of the tourists think they can look the other way on it. Except things go wrong quickly. After a horrific accident, Simon and the other tourists find themselves trapped on a tiny island in the middle of the river. It's the rainy season, and the river is rising. The island is surrounded by hungry bull sharks that won't let them swim away. And worst of all, the sharks might not be the only blood-thirsty killers among them. It was supposed to be the trip of a lifetime. Instead, they'll be lucky if they make it out with their lives at all.

DARK WATERS
by Lucas Pederson

Jörmungandr is an ancient Norse sea monster. Thought to be purely a myth until a battleship is torn a part by one.

With his brother on that ship, former Navy Seal and deep-sea diver, Miles Raine, sets out on a personal vendetta against the creature and hopefully save his brother. Bringing with him his old Seal team, the Dagger Points, they embark on a mission that might very well be their last.

But what happens when the hunters become the hunted and the dark waters reveal more than a monster?

Printed in Great Britain
by Amazon